ALSO BY CYNTHIA ZARIN

FICTION

*Inverno*

POETRY

*The Swordfish Tooth*
*Fire Lyric*
*The Watercourse*
*The Ada Poems*
*Orbit*
*Next Day: New and Selected Poems*

NONFICTION

*An Enlarged Heart: A Personal History*
*Two Cities*

CHILDREN'S BOOKS

*Rose and Sebastian*
*What Do You See When You Shut Your Eyes?*
*Wallace Hoskins, the Boy Who Grew Down*
*Albert, the Dog Who Liked to Ride in Taxis*
*Saints Among the Anima*

ESTATE

# ESTATE

*A Novel*

## CYNTHIA ZARIN

FARRAR, STRAUS AND GIROUX
New York

Farrar, Straus and Giroux
120 Broadway, New York 10271

EU Representative: Macmillan Publishers Ireland Ltd, 1st Floor,
The Liffey Trust Centre, 117–126 Sheriff Street Upper, Dublin 1, DO1 YC43

Copyright © 2025 by Cynthia Zarin
All rights reserved
Printed in the United States of America
First edition, 2025

Sun ornament by Onabi/Shutterstock.com.

Owing to limitations of space, all acknowledgments for permission to reprint previously published material can be found on page 133.

Library of Congress Cataloging-in-Publication Data
Names: Zarin, Cynthia author
Title: Estate : a novel / Cynthia Zarin.
Description: First edition. | New York : Farrar, Straus and Giroux, 2025.
Identifiers: LCCN 2025027585 | ISBN 9780374610166 hardcover
Subjects: LCGFT: Romance fiction | Novels | Fiction
Classification: LCC PS3576.A69 E88 2025 | DDC 813/.54—dc23/eng/20250609
LC record available at https://lccn.loc.gov/2025027585

Designed by Patrice Sheridan

The publisher of this book does not authorize the use or reproduction of any part of this book in any manner for the purpose of training artificial intelligence technologies or systems. The publisher of this book expressly reserves this book from the Text and Data Mining exception in accordance with Article 4(3) of the European Union Digital Single Market Directive 2019/790.

Our books may be purchased in bulk for specialty retail/wholesale, literacy, corporate/premium, educational, and subscription box use. Please contact MacmillanSpecialMarkets@macmillan.com.

www.fsgbooks.com
Follow us on social media at @fsgbooks

10 9 8 7 6 5 4 3 2 1

This is a work of fiction. Names, characters, places, organizations, and incidents either are products of the author's imagination or are used fictitiously.

FOR KAREN PRAGER BALLIETT

*Sotto dura Staggion dal sole accesa*
*Langue l'huomo, langue 'l gregge, ed arde il pino;*
*Scioglie il cucco la voce, e tosto intesa*
*Canta la tortorella e'l gardelino*
*Zeffiro dolce spira, mà contesa*
*Muove borea iproviso al suo vicino*
*E piange il pastorel, perche sospesa*
*Teme fiera borasca, e'l suo destino;*
*Toglie alle membra lasse il suo riposo*
*Il timore de' lampi, e tuoni fieri*
*E de mosche, e mossoni il stuol furioso.*
*Ah che pur troppo i suo timor son veri*
*Tuona e fulmina il ciel e grandioso*
*Tronca il capo alle spiche e a'grani alteri.*

Under the heat of the burning summer sun,
rest the shepherd and his flock; the pine is parched.
The cuckoo finds its voice, and suddenly,
the turtledove and goldfinch sing.
A gentle breeze blows,
but now the north wind appears.
The shepherd weeps because, overhead,
lies the fierce storm, and his destiny.
His tired limbs are deprived of rest
by his fear of lightning and fierce thunder,
and furious swarms of flies and hornets.
Alas, how just are his fears,
thunder and lightning fill the heavens, and the hail
breaks off the ears of proudly standing wheat.

—ANTONIO VIVALDI, "L'ESTATE,"
*LE QUATTRO STAGIONE*

ESTATE

> Sentences in which I have tried for a certain light tone—many of those have to do with events, upheavals, destructions that caused me to weep like a child.
>
> —ELIZABETH HARDWICK

I HAD BEGUN WRITING a long letter, a letter to a man with whom I was in love, at first to tell him what my days were like when he was not with me, which was most of the time, but really, to keep track of them and to convince myself that I had a life without him; and then I kept at the letter, writing every night, over a number of months, as spring turned into summer, because I felt that in the end I would have nothing else to show for abasing myself. What had started as a lark had become something else for me. I was married, but I was separated from my husband and had become involved with someone else, someone I had known for many years, and the man with whom I had now fallen inconveniently in love was claimed by not one but two other women. As usual, feinting the truth, for a short time I pretended the situation was otherwise: first, I thought I would not become attached to him, and then, after almost no time had passed, I believed I could convince him to love only me. To me then—and even now, despite my knowing better—love meant what I had run away from not once but twice: a life among towels and tablecloths and children, a solution to an algorithm

I'd tested since I was a little girl. My childhood had been one of deprivation—my mother took little notice of me, and my father was at once peremptory and prone to scenes of emotional violence. But we, I was sure, would be happy.

Later, it was pointed out to me that this was a kind of hubris. Why should Lorenzo hop on one leg, when he preferred a three-legged stool? After a while it became a letter that I did not plan to send, about which he occasionally made comments (I had told him about it), in which we spoke to each other. I recorded my daily life, and the times that we saw and more often did not see each other. Occasionally, I read bits of it aloud to him. By the time I began reading aloud, we knew each other well. Sometimes we played a game in which we spoke in each other's voices, and it was often difficult, when I looked back on what I had recorded, to know who was speaking. Many of the conversations I recorded were imagined, but that is the way in all love affairs: what one person says and what another person hears are often two different things. Much later he would say that I had fallen in love with an entirely different person, whom I had invented. But why, then, that particular invention? In time because I wanted to understand, or thought I might better understand, how I had become the person who might write such a letter, and behave in such a way, behavior of which I deeply disapproved—telephone calls late at night, or worse, no telephone call at all, keeping my toothbrush in my handbag, avoiding certain street corners, telling lies.

I also knew one of the other women, though not well, and there was that, too. I had grown up in a time when we thought darkly of what we called betrayal. I also, like Scheherazade, began to tell him a number of long stories, or tales, and to record the stories he told me. Again, some of these were true and some of them were not. For the most part they were stories in which idiotic dangers were apparent to everyone but me, or conversely, showed off his, or my own, charming vulnerability. One or several were fairy tales. Some were stories about people who disappeared, by water or by fire, or into thin air; one was about a woman caught in a snow globe. At the time I did not see the correspondences among those stories. I did, later. I thought then if I told these stories, I would unravel the length of thread that led to . . . I want to say the Minotaur's lair, but as always, in a maze, there is more than one way to lose one's way. And even if that was the case, I was mistaken. If you tell stories to a Minotaur, you should not be surprised if he doesn't wait to hear how they end.

When did I become interested in disappearance? In November 1961, Michael Rockefeller, the son of the then governor of New York, age twenty-three, vanished in New Guinea when his catamaran capsized and he drowned while trying to swim to shore. Or did he drown? His body was never found. How could that be? A story lurking in the mind's eye, a helicopter propeller over the river. He was a boy who loved beautiful things, and he had found them there, living among the Asmat people. Some of these were dugout canoes, made of nutmeg wood; others, called Bis poles, were intricately carved, made of trees that were stripped of their bark and turned upside down so the carved roots delicately scraped the air. In New York, the galleries of the Metropolitan Museum established by his bereaved family to commemorate his disappearance were a recourse at the museum with the children when I felt I couldn't look at the halls of Arms and Armor or the pond in the Chinese garden one more time. In the Chinese garden, the children had named the fish—the black-and-white one, the orange one with the red nose—and though now those names elude me, I used to pray that they would live forever, those fish. Last weekend, we were at the museum again. Sunday came around, everyone was bored, and again it was raining. To enter the Michael C. Rockefeller Wing you turn left, past the Fabergé eggs and gilt snuffboxes, the tiny walnut that opens like the nutshell in the fairy tale, and a whale mask from British Columbia the size of a dogfish, with its open mouth set on hinges. Just today, a lobsterman on the East Coast of America was swallowed by a whale, and spit out again. We were on our way to the cafeteria for cake. Next to the elevator was a show of John Marin drawings, and I recalled decades ago driving down to find Cape Split in Maine, where he had lived. There was a hobbyhorse in the bent grass by one falling-down house, which was the same hobbyhorse we'd had as children, made out of some kind of molded plastic, a chestnut horse with a white face. There were nicks in the painted hide where I had picked at it to see what the horse was made of underneath. Here in Cape Split was the identical horse, in the beaten-down yard by a trailer. There must have been hundreds of them made, a stable of hobbyhorses, and one had ended up in the basement of our house in Massachusetts. My brothers and I took turns riding it, and I can still feel the hard saddle pushing the seam of my red overalls between my legs, and smell the cold plastic when I stroked my cheek on the horse's brow as if it were alive. What happened to the horse? Absence is so much easier to love.

As I wrote the letter, I addressed you in the second person, as one does. It was the only time I could be sure you were listening. Here's a little place marker: Tarquinia. I am thinking of the first story you told me, in the kitchen that night after Pablo's birthday party, when you stayed to help me clean up.

## ESTATE

You were Pablo's friend, and he asked if you might be invited. It was January. Before that, although we had met now and again, we had not talked together, alone. There were candles in the kitchen and piles of plates. (Now, in your mirrored kitchen, it is impossible for me to not at least rinse the plates, despite your chiding.) That night you told me the story of Antonella. Is that her name, or was she someone else—a similar story? A cinematic story: a man very much like you, but younger, but not so young, thirty, perhaps, goes to a wedding. He does not know the groom well, and the bride not at all; the invitation was sent to a friend, who invited him to come along, but the friend is ill, or unexpectedly called away, but he himself goes anyway. It's late spring, the pink oleanders are in bloom, it isn't far from Rome, where he lives. Even the car park smells of jasmine. He is a theater director in the middle of rehearsals, but it is Saturday. He has had a headache all week, but perhaps if he gets out of Rome he'll feel better. He is seeing someone, he is always seeing someone; he is a man who is attractive to women because he has beautiful eyes, the color of—even now I hear your voice, what does it matter what color they were?—and he seems sad, as though he is reaching always for something in himself that he cannot find, and of course the women feel they can supply it, and he has a way of just brushing their shoulders with an index finger. His aunt has a house outside Tarquinia; he visits her often, so the car knows the way. He is the kind of man who pays careful attention to elderly relatives. His mother is alive, but his father is dead. He himself is abstracted, thinking about the second lead. It was stupid, to cast someone because you felt a little sorry for them. It was warm, the wedding was outside on the large patio of the villa. Tables were spread out below with white cloths in a clearing before the wood. Was it spring or had it turned into summer? I don't remember.

During the ceremony the bride kept her eyes down. Because he was standing off at a little distance, he did not see her face properly until the reception. By then, because a breeze had come up, she was wearing a white cashmere shawl over her dress, which was made of lace rosettes. There was a small mark on the inside of her arm above the elbow where the side zipper had snagged her skin earlier. He had been on the outskirts of the melee around her, but then he found himself at her side. Because her glass was empty, he asked if he could refill it for her, and when she said yes, he introduced himself, saying his name and that he was a friend of ———, who was unable to come, but as it was a beautiful day, he had come to wish her well, and he hoped that was permissible. As always, his courtesy was old-fashioned and slightly otherworldly.

She was a singer. Later, there would be other singers. Or perhaps she was not the first one. She was getting married, but she did not want to get married; she did not know why she had done this—it was lunacy, getting married; she wished she was wearing something other than this stupid dress; she did not love this man who seemed now almost surreally to be her husband. It was a mistake, wasn't it, if she was feeling like this? He seemed to understand, yes? How had it happened, this conversation? It was cool under the trees. It was June, but in the shade the pine needles clung to their scent of autumn and salt. Improbably, by walking just a short way together, they had disappeared into an enchanted wood. He was at once bewitched and preening a little. Despite his usual feeling that the world was having a dream in which he was a figure dreamed up by someone else, because, after all, although he was generally successful with women with barely any effort, the reverse of effort, which he had found earlier than most, suited him, a kind of languorous distraction, it is unusual to seduce a bride at a wedding. Her willingness, the atmosphere of fracas, her feeling of doom, of having made the wrong decision, had propelled her under the trees. Sometime later he drove back to Rome.

Over the next months, into the fall, she called from wherever she was singing. She had an accompanist, and they traveled together. There were all kinds of contretemps with the accompanist, with her mother, with the food in hotels, she lost her luggage at every stop, she had laryngitis and whispered into the phone to save her voice. About five months later, before Christmas, she called and talked more wildly than usual; when he asked where she was, she said that she was downstairs, in the phone booth on the street below his apartment. He let her in. When Stefano was born, she registered the baby under the name of her husband. At first she refused to let him see the baby, then she relented. By then she had separated from her husband, she was angry because he himself would not marry her, he began traveling back and forth from São Paolo, where he now lived, where he directed a theater company, in order to see the baby, which was deranging and expensive. Under the influence of this detestable mother, whom he now despised, the child developed habits of mind of which he did not approve, a tendency to hysteria, to disorder, that led later to missing planes and losing luggage, getting a ticket for riding a bicycle on the sidewalk. Like him the child grew up in Italy and then went to school in New York, and had keys to many apartments, and a tendency to disappear.

Do you remember that this was the first story you told me? That evening you told me, I turned from the sink where I was stacking the plates, and rested my arm against the porcelain ledge, and turned so that the inside of my wrist was visible to you, and then withdrew it. You told me that, later. Did you tell me the story then? The story of a man who embarks on an affair with a woman at her wedding, who is then pursued by that woman, who has a child whom he tries to take away from her, a child he did not want but nonetheless pursues, whom he loves, who confounds and irritates him, and later terrifies him and becomes the only person on earth who has a hold on him. A boy who likes vegetables and butterflies and money. A woman who is demanding and hysterical. To a close reader, which I was not, the story was a warning, or a map. Which was it? It began with a disappearance into a wood.

The first night we had dinner, it was raining. But we had already met in the rain—it was raining that night, the week before, when we'd met for a drink, which followed a coffee the previous week, two months after you returned from Corfu, where you had been making the film for which you are now recording the voice-over. Sometimes I think that the weeks that spring were cloaked with rain. We met at the ratty Café du Bois, where I go often with the children, who eat the spaghetti, and until that afternoon, after which I got up from the table and went home to fix supper, you were still part of that world, making the children laugh, coming to parties at the house with Esther, with whom you were living or not living, where we met quite casually, barely taking notice of each other except for one or two small incidents, a hem slightly raised, a touch. It was at that drink that you told me that there was a second woman, who lived in ———. She came to New York for a month here, a month there. Did it predate your years with Esther? Perhaps. That I don't remember. She was married, her life was a mess; no, you did not want her to leave her husband. Once, a few years earlier, you had written

ESTATE 11

to me that you were in Stockholm, and the afternoon light was coming in the window, a fog light, and you were reading a book. I was surprised to hear from you. Perhaps that is where she lived then. Now she lives in Prague. And then when you came back and you were at the house for a party, I showed you the picture that my grandfather had painted of my grandmother that hangs between the windows of my bedroom, in which she is sitting in an Adirondack chair on a lawn bordered by what look like cypresses. It was upstate New York; there were no cypresses. They must be fir trees. The sky is full of thunderheads. I showed you how my grandfather had painted the wooden frame the exact color of the sky, so that the picture extends into the frame that holds it, and colors what lies beyond it. I had loved that picture, and before she died my grandmother gave it to me. It struck me then as you looked at the picture that you were capable of tenderness. I thought so, but it isn't true. Or at least there is a place, not far from where that thought starts, where it stops. In the picture my grandmother is wearing a dress that is identical in cut to the one your mother is wearing in Venice in a snapshot you later showed me. She is standing by the Accademia Bridge. It is the same time, the early sixties. You showed me the photograph because the dress that I wore one night was a similar dress. Sleeveless, brown wool, to the knee, with a few flat bows sewn onto the seams. There are no photographs on the walls or tables in your apartment. You had to fetch the photograph from a drawer in the study.

Later you found a hanger and hung up my dress so it would not crease. Your mother was tall, taller than I am. I would not have thought that. She was rangy the way some women were then, all legs and smoke, her dark hair cut so it swings at the chin. I never met your mother, although perhaps I did, in the elevator of the apartment building on Park Avenue where I visited my cousins, and where you lived with her and your sister when you came to live in New York in the seventies. In the bar the other day, when you began to describe that apartment, I felt the map of the world closing in, a tug on a string, and I knew before you named the address that it was the building where my cousins lived, and where I often came for the weekend. The elevator walls were green. It turns out that as children we had the same sense of odd pleasure: the address was on the avenue, but you entered the building on a side street, under the dark green awning that all buildings of a certain type have in New York. Your mother had grown up in New York, not far from the address to which she returned. Months later, after an evening when you had taken me home—from the street the house looked like a ship, every window lit, the children upstairs—you said you could not stay, that you were expected elsewhere. Later, you told me that after I had disappeared inside, you had circled the block three or four times, willing yourself to ring the bell and come in, but you could not do it.

The other day, because that is what we do now, I found pictures of another of your singers on the Internet, and listened to her sing, onstage in smoke and then alone, wearing almost nothing, in what I feel sure is your apartment, backed up against the moldings that are particular to buildings of a certain age on the Upper West Side. A face that launched a thousand ships. Who left, but not entirely, leaving a shadow of herself in the doorway. A sleeve turned inside out, a dugout canoe, because when what is between two people departs, it is like a person gone missing.

Years ago, when I was still married, although my husband and I had grown distant, we went after the New Year to Santa

Fe, and on Epiphany we were taken up into the hills to see the Three Kings Dance. It was snowing. The elders danced in the carcasses of eagles, their faces painted blue. At that point I was preoccupied with someone else, whom I had loved since I was very young, who had recently reappeared in my life and hollowed it out so I could find nothing good in what was left, an eon of time in which it was always snowing; a story about which I later told you a great deal, but not everything. Because it was January, the dark began to ink the corners of the pueblo early, and when the moon rose it was printed with the face of my friend, and his reflection was written in turn on mine. His name was Alastair. You like to think that what you feel is written on your face—that you are simple and shy and easy to read. The opposite is true, and you like that better. The other morning when you left me at the subway after we had spent the night together, you spoke for a few minutes in the lobby with your friend the baroness, who is ninety-seven—you are the kind of man who collects elderly baronesses, like a jazz player or a priest—and later you told me that she called in the evening to say she had had an erotic dream about you.

At the first dinner we had together, in that terrible restaurant, you showed me a pair of dice that you had had made, for a friend who was a jazz musician, who was dying. They were made out of some kind of alloy, and heavy to hold, heavier than you would expect, really. The dice are one of the only things I remember about that dinner. It was raining that night, and I had a hard time finding a cab. I texted you to say I was late—but I did not have your cell phone number then, and the text bounced back, because the number was a landline—and when I got to the restaurant, it was packed and full of wet overcoats and a few large parties. A blustery Friday night in the West

Seventies. We changed tables, finally, to a corner where it was not so loud. I think the dice were made of brass? You had had them cast according to his directions: each side of the die had not a number but a musical note, so that when the player would "roll the dice," the musical sentences would be dictated by the die, an infinite array of melodies, a tarot pack of sound. They were nice to hold in the hand. I was moved by the idea of your going to different metalsmiths to have them made. The last set, you said, were too light. There were small candles on the table. The brass dice reflected little shots of light. What did we talk about? I think I asked about your father. You seemed to me in that moment a man of great tenderness surrounded by the spirits of the dead.

I was late. After that I was always late to meet you. I didn't know then that your friends are almost always sick or dying, often on another continent, and that the great flourishing of friendship almost always happened years ago. Or that your preoccupation is with people who are at some remove. It didn't strike me that I am like that, too. In the time we were together, if that is what I can call it, I only met one or two of your friends, and now one of them is dead. I have met one or two relatives, fleetingly. Your son, of course, though why I say of course I don't know; your sister, with her face like a cameo; later, your cousins in Rome. In the taxi on the way to meet you, it was as if fireflies were pricking the surface of my skin. I am beginning to forget what I have told you and what I have not—although that is not entirely true, as I wish I had told you more, or you had told me more, but together we do so little talking. Years later, just the other night, in the garden—I had just returned from a week away—I said, it is odd that we tell each other so little, and you said, but what does that have to do with anything?

Fireflies pricking the surface of my skin. One evening years ago, outside Vicenza, I visited friends who had taken a house there for the summer, a couple I had known for many years, Daniel and Naomi. Later, he went mad. We were sitting on the patio which looked out on the road that wound through the hills, and one side of the hill was lit with fireflies. There were so many, they looked like fairy lights. But the other side of the road was in darkness. I can't remember now—which side of the road was olives, and which was grapes? That's what I was told, olives or grapes. Which did the fireflies love? I have never wanted to know. I have carried this image so long that it has folded in the middle, like a book in which one page mirrors the facing page; the black field on one side, the fireflies studding the dark on the other. It's the demarcation that interests me, the line between the two. One, or the other. At least once I've dreamed of that road.

The food was terrible. I remember wondering what we were doing there—why you had picked that restaurant. I thought later it was because it was near your apartment. I did know that to meet for supper on a Friday was different than meeting for coffee on a Wednesday afternoon or a drink on a Thursday. I wondered vaguely where Esther was that evening—your arrangements were not clear to me. Nor are they now, many years later. Though that is not entirely true: I know what is possible, and what is not. But even now, I can hear you saying, don't be so sure. Between the drink and our dinner, a week had elapsed, and in between those meetings we had met again at a dinner party. I was uneasy. I liked Esther, and although we were not really friends, I did not like knowing something that she did not. It occurs to me now that she perhaps knew all along, about Valeria, and later, she also knew about me—that the deception was an elaborate ruse for my benefit. At the Café du Bois you had told me you had been involved with Valeria for two years. Or four years. Or ten years. The number keeps changing. That you had been seeing Valeria for half the time you've been with Esther. I thought that at our rainy dinner we would continue that conversation. We did not. And, with certain exceptions, we have not spoken of it again, although in Rome last summer, almost ten years later, I did ask about Valeria, who like Esther as usual is unwell; her ailments, never life-threatening, always have a tinge of the medieval; she is flat on her back, her blood is being drawn. The women seemed to me so like each other, it made little difference.

And of course, I was different. Or so I thought, in my almost complete self-delusion. But even I was aware that my dispassionate feelings could change in an instant, and so they did. But then, the only time I felt real jealousy was at a party when you spoke for a long time to Eloise, who is only an acquaintance, a friend of friends, as I had been, one leg crossed over the other, and your glasses, which you generally do not wear, sliding down your nose; she was leaning forward eagerly to illustrate a point, and you were clearly engaged and happy in the sound of her voice. We were avoiding each other that evening.

Do you remember that morning you did not help me on with my coat as we were all leaving Pablo's mother's funeral, a coat you had not seen before, as I had arrived before you, but you had fetched anyway, knowing instantly it was mine—a leather coat, with a double row of buttons—and almost threw it at me? It was the only time, a few weeks after it began, that I had seen you rattled. You told me later that you did not dare to look at me for fear it would show on your face. When I went down the hall to the bathroom, you followed me and said only, *ti sei tagliato i capelli*, and your voice fell in the small room, a child's abandoned room, with the posters of rock musicians still taped to the wall, as if you had parted my legs and slipped in your tongue.

There is the secret life we are living and the secret life of these sentences, my knowledge as I write them that I have parsed out the words, seven hundred per day: when I get to one hundred days, this will be finished. But even I know we know much less about the experiences we have than those we do not; about what has failed to happen, or could have happened— about this we are experts. Last night you brought flowers, a huge bouquet of roses and rubrum lilies, and this morning I cut the stems and put them in vases around the house. At the bar the other night you asked me what it was called in English— forsythia; the banks of yellow now open along the drives in the park. You knew, I am sure. In Italian is it *ginestra*? That is broom. I will ask you today, in the car. One hundred days from now it will be almost autumn.

A day by the beach. The word I learned in Italian is *nascondino*: hide-and-seek. And you learned "devil's pocketbook," for the black sea pouches that wash up on the ocean here, which you do not have on the Mediterranean. It was cold on the beach. It was twenty-four hours in which the minutes slowed down and grew, like the garden in a plastic pouch we had as children—or at least I did; it is hard for me to imagine, really, your childhood because my tendency is to romanticize everything in a gold light, smelling of lavender and bay leaves, but perhaps it was something like that. Party favors: a plastic bag with what looked like nothing, a dried pebble, at the bottom; when you followed the instructions on the little piece of paper that came attached to the bag—

JUST ADD WATER AND SEE YOUR GARDEN GROW

—there it was, a pink flower or a tiny shrub with leaves. A devil's pocketbook. Were the flowers real? Did it matter? I wonder where it comes from, this search for surprise, for love, constant as the search for lost keys before going out the door. The stories you tell make more sense to me than the story of your life now, or mine; we avoid these subjects assiduously as if we are tenderly and tactfully avoiding discussing a malady or a secret vice that belongs to someone else we both know well. When you and your sister, Susanna, were little, in Bevagna, she woke you up every night. She wanted you to accompany her to the bathroom. The boy warm in the bed, tousled by sleep, dreaming— I imagine you are warm because you are almost always warm now—woken with a pull on the bedclothes by a girl just slightly larger. You were so sleepy that you fell asleep sitting on the floor outside the bathroom, and woke when the toilet flushed. She was afraid of the dark.

Here is the second story, also in Bevagna. A family had moved to Italy from New Mexico, and the little girl became a friend of Susanna's. It was a rainy afternoon, and you played *nascondino*. During the game of hide-and-seek you took the little girl deep into a closet, and although your sister and her friends searched, opening the closet door, you eluded discovery. Because of your mother, you knew a little English. It was probably half an hour, there in the folded dream. You were kissing when they found you. You were six. As I said, all your stories are about girls. When the girls grow up, they are women who are a little crazy, a little dependent, full of alibis. Always a mishap, a hurt, a trouble, as if the inner distress is translated onto the body. Perhaps because I have children, I do not want anymore to be anyone's child. At least that is what I thought; it wasn't as clear to me then how these categories—mother, child—transpose themselves; the head of a bull on the body of a man. The first night in that terrible restaurant in the rain when I was late and you showed me the dice, I asked you a question—I asked you on Sunday in Montauk, again—but I do not remember what you said. The other morning before we left your apartment, I was reading or trying to read *The Duino Elegies*, which I had left open on the shelf, words drifting up off the page. *Jeder Engel ist schrecklich*. It was the Third Elegy, the boy looking for love in every crease. On the opposite page, *Ogni angelo è terribile*. What I asked was, what are we doing here?

And you said, there are some things that happen you cannot take back. You are caustic, as if the words burned your mouth. The restaurant was on Seventieth Street, and when we left, we crossed the river of Seventy-Second Street, the lights of the cars reflecting on the wet street, and the freezing rain catching in my fur hat. We were out in our boat. We were crossing to the other side—did you know that yet? A few weeks ago, you said to me that you did not know then if the first time would be the last time—just that once—but I think it is one of the only times (though how can I know, we are both liars) that you lied to me. But one rarely thinks: this is the last time. One starts off wanting to tell the truth.

When years ago I could not go home, when I first met Alastair, again, and could not see for crying in the car, I would pull to the side of the road, like a parent who says to a child, we will not go any farther unless you behave. Those were the days when I drove the Renault, and it kept breaking down, because nothing was ever fixed properly, and then whatever it was—cars, ceilings, tables, love—would collapse under its own weight, the way things become heavier when you are tired of carrying them. In the apartment we had then, where I lived with my husband and children, there was an icebox that dripped water into the vegetable bins, where it would then freeze. In those days I cooked pasta and baked chicken and meatloaf for the children, and then I would make a separate supper, veal stew, or omelets, or coq au vin, to eat later. It is hard to imagine now, what we sat and talked about: I can't, really. What did we say, I wonder? It vanishes like dew, like mist. In those days, too, there was a lightbulb in the door of the freezer. I think I have told you about it. Perhaps one of the children put it there. They were small. What happens when you freeze light? they asked. I remember a long conversation about what the speed of light could mean and where it went. Sunlight to them seemed as permanent as the light fixture in the kitchen, and they resisted the idea that something that belonged to them had to travel to get where they were. The lightbulb—I think it was a 60-watt bulb— stayed in the freezer for a decade, until we moved to this house. I regret throwing it away. This morning you wrote that you were going out into the day but taking me with you. You like that image and often use it. It is not something I think about. When I am on my own, I feel unaccompanied. And, it is irritating: if you'd like me to come with you, ask me. But that imaginary person is perhaps a better companion? Yesterday, I felt your eye on me while a student sat in my office weeping, and as I stretched, I felt your hand run along my shoulder. You often keep still and move your thumb slowly on the small of my back. Was that something my skin knew, that day you put me in the taxi? I was getting Pom from school, and you were waiting for the bus with me, which did not come. You hailed a taxi and told the driver the school address—how did you know it?—and it felt as if you had put me in a taxi a hundred times. Which then turned out to be true. How many times, exactly?

There are some things you can't undo. Earlier in the day, it was November 17, 1961, in Kiunga in the North Fly District, Michael Rockefeller and a Dutch anthropologist, René Wassing, set off in a twelve-meter-long catamaran, made of a raft slung between two dugout canoes. It was a calm day. In the morning, the colloquy among the birds—the cassowaries, which do not leave the ground, the turkeys, the grey teal—said that today it would not rain. It did not rain. But the sea picked up. If they had known, if the birds had said *don't go*, if the sky had issued a warning? It did not. A boat from a hollowed tree. A dragon boat; a legend: a man was in love with his sister, and was banished by his people, the sea-nomads, to float without end in a dugout canoe. An old story, to want to cross the river. An old story, to think you know otherwise. "I am having a most exhausting but thoroughly enjoyable time here," Michael wrote to his father. Later, a man I loved would disappear after playing a game of Risk. Another, after setting up a table in the garden. I'll do that, he said. Gone. Later you would say, you could have called me. To finish the table? Even here, where I sit in a garden a hundred yards from the Tiber, ten years later, you write this morning and say, I'll call you later. A river of ash. He thought he could swim to shore.

Notes for a novel: he was a man who liked women who did not have children, but now, two of the women he loves have children, while a third wants to have a child. Mine are always with me, their hands on me, even now when she is tired and we are reading in bed, Pom will slip her hand into the neck of my blouse, her lips moving. Even George relaxes as he sits very close to me. Sometimes, very late at night, he comes in when he is home from school and gets into bed with me. Tell me, I say. Listen, Mama, you are not listening, Louie complains. I remember asking you if Valeria was planning to leave her husband, and you said with irritation, I don't know, shaking your head. It is not a question I would ask now. The other afternoon when it was getting time for you to leave, I pulled your pink-and-white-striped shirt from the chair and put it on. I was cold. But I had been eyeing that shirt for a while, and wanted my bare skin inside it. For a small man you have broad shoulders, and the shirt was big on me.

In the apartment on Park Avenue where you lived with your mother and sister, and where I visited my cousins, the elevator walls were made of worn green leatherette, and I would surreptitiously peel it off with my finger, and now it turns out you did this, too. I didn't know then that it was an apartment full of stories, some of which, later, I would learn by heart, as if the words on those pages lingered in the charred air like smoke from an imaginary cigar. We worked at each other's depredations even then. I don't remember the elevator being attended. Now, when we are together, it is a little like being in an elevator, the sudden and strange intimacy that vanishes when the door opens. Like your apartment, to which everyone has a key. For a man who does not like to be surprised, why do you give out so many keys?

That is the question: what am I doing, more or less? In the end, as so often happens, the thing that seemed essential is not, and what turns out to hold the world together is a lightbulb with a skin of ice. But I was not then thinking about the life I had pieced together, or what it entailed. It would have surprised me that I would think about that all the time, later on, when wherever I went things would explode out of my handbag: coins, keys, a pair of glasses, crumpled tissues, because I was trying to hold too much at once. Years later, by the Boat Pond—it was one of the last times I saw you before we saw each other again—we noticed that the red light stayed longest on the water, with only a moment of green; a reflection of the stoplights on the Park Drive. The last time until now, that is. It was almost summer. We sat on a blanket, six feet apart, wearing only light sweaters, you at one corner of the striped blanket I had brought, and I at the other. It was the first spring of the plague. You said, we have tried everything else, perhaps we should live together this summer. Is it necessary to report that we did not? Once you thought that the first time would be the only time, but as I said, that wasn't true. During that time, when we first began to see each other, a man I knew went mad, a man of strong opinions. Afterward, his wife's father, who by then sometimes recognized her but often not, would sometimes say, as the day drew in, "It was sad that man who died in the fire." And she would say, "Yes, Daddy, it was sad." A man who loses his mind, who dies the day after his children have come to visit him for lunch. They played Risk. For a long time, I thought—suicide, death by drowning, by fire, by disappearance—I thought, these cannot be things that have happened to us.

When I was at school, the professor supervising my thesis kept a box of Teuscher truffles in his desk drawer. As I remember, it was always winter, but it must have at some point been spring. I arrived in the heavy snow, in an old jacket with holes in the pockets into which coins had fallen and made a jangling sound. My hair fell to my waist, and I had barely combed it. We did not comb our hair, then. Part of the instruction he gave me, a man of exquisite manners in what I thought of as his old age—he must have been sixty-five, one of the most vigorous men I have known, crossing the street in his loden coat and beret—was to take me to lunch. We went every few weeks to a small Spanish restaurant blocks from campus. He ordered for us both: squid in ink sauce, avocado with prawns. He disregarded my slovenly hair and aggressively unkempt clothes. If he liked a sentence I had written, he would make a distinctive tsking sound. Sometimes he would point out sentences and lines in other books: *Clocks and carpets and chairs / on the lawn all day,* and

> *out of maize & air*
> *your body's made, and moves. I summon, see,*
> *from the centuries it.*
> *I think you won't stay. How do we*
> *linger, diminished, in our lovers' air,*
> *implausibly visible, to whom, a year,*
> *years, over interims; or not;*
> *to a long stranger; or not; shimmer & disappear.*

Memorize it, he said. In those years I lived in a dilapidated house in what was then a sad street in Cambridge, behind the Museum of Comparative Zoology. Somewhere there is a photograph of me and the boy I lived with then. We are standing on the small covered porch of the house, and snow covers each branch like icing sugar. Snow paints the eaves over us and dusts the clapboard under the window. The windows do not close properly. Inside the house, in the front room we shared, snow has furred the windowsills, turning the fountain pen he left on the sill into a tiny log canoe stuck in ice. Yesterday, thirty years after this picture was taken, he wrote to me, asking whether I had seen the notice of the death of a girl he remembered who was in my class. No. Evidence of his capacity for total recall and my lack of it. We lived together for three years. In the end, we parted, with rancor. He married the sister of a friend, a possessor even then of houses and bank accounts. All of it, his insistence on fountain pens, on books in alphabetical order, on not cracking the spines of those books—paperbacks!—drifts back over me, like snow that will not stop falling. It's a black-and-white photograph—in those days we only used black-and-white film. We had been precocious children, and now even our nostalgia was precocious. At twenty, we referred with wry fondness to our own impossibly faraway childhoods, seen at a great distance, dioramas inside of a disappearing perspective of small RCA TVs that had shown us the world outside the nursery in sharp-edged blacks and grays, a world on fire, full of shrapnel, a world where we could and would hurt ourselves. There was not the obsession we have now with safety; as children we hit our heads on the corners of the glass coffee tables, which were covered with ashtrays, like maps of a country studded with small volcanos. There was no help for some things, we knew. After recess, we crouched under our desks to drill for the end of the world: *like pretzels, boys and girls, like pretzels!* When did I become so interested in disappearance? Dismissed early, in the middle of the day, we came home to find our fathers, who wore their authority implacably, whom the train conductor, the doorman, the man in the moon, called Sir, in shirtsleeves, inexplicably in tears, in front of the television's shadow box, where a little girl wearing a pale blue coat stood next to her brother, who saluted his father.

Down. Gone. There were things that did not happen and things that could not be helped. At school, years later, that girl in the pale blue coat, grown up, said, I'm sure you don't remember me, we met at ———'s party, I'm Caroline. Before dawn, bolt upright on West End Avenue, listening for the end of the world, to be blown to smithereens as we knew we would be all along, I woke Alastair, the light a sprocket through the torn shade: listening for a death rattle, the sawing of a branch overhead, the sound of nocturnal women beating carpets, or so thought Betty Flanders, in *Jacob's Room*, of the guns on the French front—riveted by the whir of a plane due east, landing at LaGuardia. Weaving spiders come not here. Never saw the sun shining so bright. Daisy, Daisy, give me your answer true; under the toppled cherry tree, *I did, I did chop it with my hatchet*; the old cherry trees dreaming of all that was a hundred, two hundred years ago, oppressed by their heavy visions, said Trofimov. The whole ball of wax, the whole nine yards, the kit and kaboodle, the pink suit the French cleaners were not allowed to touch, the PT boat—our shipwreck like Jacob's shabby slipper, burnt near the water's edge where someone—when?—had built a bonfire. What were you thinking? What did Caroline say? I thought that I could make it right. What could we see from shore? A red tin can. We spent hours in the closet playing hide-and-seek.

But I was describing a photograph. If I find it, I'll show it to you, although I can see your reaction even now. You are interested in your own past, not mine. In the photograph, Thomas and I are standing on the small stoop in front of the derelict house. I am smaller and slighter than he is. I am wearing a plaid wool shirt, and he is wearing what I know to be a red-and-black wool checkered jacket. My hair, which has caught the snow, is a sheath that covers most of my white face; his hair is only a little shorter, but in the picture, you can tell it is a lighter brown. My hair then was almost black. His mouth covers mine. Who took the photograph? I have no idea.

But why do I want to look for this photograph? In the days when my marriage was ending, I hid everything remotely incendiary, and the result is that I can find almost nothing at all of the girl I was, before she became someone else: a person who arrives in the middle of the night in your immaculate apartment, with its drawings and furniture and the copy of Rilke in Italian left open on the long bookcase—a transitive verb, who became the woman walking down the grid of streets along the park, taking off her gloves, carrying a sheaf of pale orange tulips, who sees, on the table, a paper sack printed with the name of a famous chocolate shop; afterward, before we leave, you will carefully strip the bed, because more than a few people have keys to your apartment. Would they really examine the sheets? Or is this a kind of fastidiousness of yours? I would say it is a kind of fastidiousness I have noticed in small men, but you are the first small man I have known, a man who does not loom over me. When you put me in that famous taxi of ours, the moment like paper blown off a drinking straw, a thing that flies but is really nothing at all—I wish now I had kept a receipt, or noticed the driver's name. Hecate, perhaps. I sit on your beautiful red sofa and read Rilke to you like a schoolgirl. I am writing quickly, I am hundreds of words behind though I am writing every day, the word count is a spell: when I finish these pages, something will have happened. A door will open, a hole in the hedge. I must not hold on to anything too tightly—keys, houses, the smell of your cologne, you in the closet with the little girl in Bevagna, my brown dress, the lightbulb in the icebox, someone saying last night, if I hear the words *country house* as one word one more time I will scream, my leaving my handbag in the hallway and you hiding it, as if that would make a difference. In this small movie I am making, I tell no one. I think, of course, this is to avoid humiliation. But I will have to pull myself together, and stop orchestrating a kind of perfection that I know is a fetish with you, as if I were both the curator and the show, a small one of selected works, for which you have a printed ticket for a private viewing. As if once everything else disappears, I will know where I am. But I am the one who disappears.

*She stood very still in the boxwood. It had begun with a letter, two lines connected at three vertices. The lines met at the top, leaning against each other, but the third line connected them at the midpoint of the first two lines. A is for apple, said her aunt, who had been reading aloud. The letter was on the page, next to a drawing of a tree heavy with apples. There were apples on the ground where some had fallen. Her aunt left her and went inside the house. A, she said aloud. If she made herself small, she could walk under the central beam and climb up and sit under the peaked roof. It would be easier to do if the letter could be tilted. She did that. One letter after another made a word. Words made sentences. They stopped, but then they started up again. A long time later, she tried to explain it—very carefully, like a schoolgirl. She took the little leatherbound book in which he was taking notes and turned it so that the lines were vertical instead of horizontal, and the letters he had written were loops and angles, and she said that when she had learned to read and write, she had imagined it just this way: the lines of letters were like logs of a raft in the water, and she was running from one end of the raft to the other. She knew it was up to her; she knew to keep the craft steady, a task she knew had been given to her that she must keep at forever.*

*She could not stop, or she would slip in between the lashings. Her father had a typewriter, her fingers fit the keys in the little hollows where the letters were printed.* Royal *it said. There was the A, the small a—a snail, or a balloon with a tail, a head bowed over a carriage. There was a lever to move the carriage. It was marked* Return. *Don't bang the keys, he said. She stood still, in the boxwood, in a declivity by the door. Wait, her aunt said. The tiny leaves just fit onto her fingertips. She was a tiny Alice, tiny as the bad fairy in Sleeping Beauty, seen through the wrong end of the telescope, with her minuscule black shoes, her sawtooth black silk, her broomstick the bar of a trapeze swing attached to the wire that came down from the circus big top. A series of lines and circuits. How unhappy the bad fairy is to be uninvited! You can tell she is unhappy; she stamps her tiny foot, no bigger than a beetle. The keys of the typewriter were like spider legs. Bang went the keys, jamming. She could take them apart, one by one. Be careful with that! her father said. A was for Alice, but C was for Caroline, a fingernail moon. You can write your name, her aunt had said. A pie with a piece cut out. Between them, B on its side, an arched edge at the end of the garden. B was a sting. The letters can spell* yes *but they can also spell* no: *to cast a spell was to make a wish. She was spellbound in the boxwood, in the declivity by the stone stairs. Somewhere else in the maze of the hedge were her bits of string, her rabbit's foot, the bookplate buried under a flat stone, the tiny bird skeleton, a gum wrapper, but for now she is spellbound, the black lines of the page on the white ground veering away and down. A letter is something to send in the mail. The C with a curve cut out. Later pi, irrational. A notebook, spiral-bound. What is missing? What is left? Hold on, hold on, said Alastair, as they veered toward the tree, the sled skidding, the runners writing on the ice where the grass would be green in summer.*

*They were children. What is love? 'Tis not hereafter. Now it was summer. "You can't keep banging your head against reality and saying it isn't there." Headhunters hunt heads. Can you canoe? Be my . . . little baby—hold on tight. In* Spellbound, *the line of threads on the white counterpane is the stuff of bad dreams. Charles Kane says, I run a couple of newspapers. What do you do? Does she know about the sled? said her father. Can you hold? asked the operator. Is Pop governor yet? Not yet, Junior. The world about to go to pieces. All around her is the drone of bees.*

---

I can hold on now only to Pom. The rest of them have already taken what they need from me. The other morning, because I drink it so quickly, the coffee does not have time to go stale, because coffee is not one of the things, I tell myself, that I care about, about which I make my life difficult, I do not grind the coffee—and because I was afraid the coffee machine would play its tricks (as it did this morning, leaking water and coffee from an unidentifiable place in the mechanism), I pulled out the French press and boiled the water in the stained but beautiful teakettle which is by now totally impractical. Years ago, it was only somewhat impractical. It does not whistle—which I like, as the sound of a teakettle whistling always sounds desperate to me—but the square, elegant handle gets very hot, and you must use a mitt to pour the boiling water into the pot or cup.

Now, what's more, it leaks. The stove in the kitchen is vast, and the little bit of water in the kettle leaked and caused a rust spot or pool of water on the griddle—but so many things in the kitchen cause water spills and rust that only when George pointed out that the kettle was sitting in a pool of water did I notice it. It is the kind of thing he notices. I think it leaks because it has been left to boil out too often, and over time the heat has made a hole in the bottom. It is impossible to see the hole, dear Liza, the hole in the bucket. Then fix it, dear Henry. Somehow along the way I have become both Liza and Henry. Shall I note here that you know this, and bought me a replacement for this kettle? The same one, at great expense.

That morning, I burned myself trying to make coffee in the French press. After the kettle boiled (the new one, which you supplied from God knows where, *un negozio nell'aria*), I put too much water in the glass cylinder, and when I pressed down, hot water and coffee grounds spewed over the counter, onto the green tiles that edge the vegetable sink, onto the floor. The hot water splashed on the inside of my left forearm and onto my chest. I was wearing a thick sweater over a T-shirt, and while the sweater is stained, I am wearing it anyway, as I type this—I have not washed it, as lately I have not done so many things. It is an ugly, checkered brown-and-red sweater. At first the burn didn't hurt. I did know enough to put my arm under cold water, which I did at the double sink. The water hissed on my arm. The swan-neck tap, with its two silver wings. That should have been a warning, but as it did not hurt immediately, I did not recognize it. Even once it began to hurt, I did not hold it under running water long enough. I wanted to make more coffee before Naomi, who was staying in the house for a few days, came down for breakfast. I had an almost perverse desire to please her. So my attention was taken up with wiping off the counter and the tiles, and remaking the coffee. She did come down, her red hair just washed and wrapped in a towel. Or I think I did not remake it, as the coffee left in the press was perfectly good. And now that I reread this, I remember that I did not tell her about the burn, as it was her husband who had set himself on fire.

    I am guiding my mind back to the burn, as one would coax a dog or a child, a child who keeps picking at holes in a fence with a stick she has broken off from a shrub, the white end oozing a little sap, the clean smell of wood, the exciting feeling, almost erotic, of having altered the world just slightly. The branch was intact before she tore it off with her hand, walking a few steps behind her mother, who has no idea of the violence she is capable of at six. If she could she would gnaw at the stick with her teeth. The burn was at first bright red, the color of a sunburn, but defined, as if I had burned myself by focusing a magnifying glass on the inside of my arm a few inches from the wrist. The burn is the shape of Australia. On the first day it stayed bright red, and it hurt a little, but I thought nothing of it. I burn myself often. One of the first times I woke up in your cavernous apartment, the curtains pulled over the bow window, and the light as always gray, as if in these rooms it is always raining, the ceiling mother-of-pearl, you said, it is better. I had badly burned a knuckle on my left hand, cooking. That was, I understand now, by looking at pictures of scarifying burns on the Internet, a second-degree burn, because it blistered. For a number of days, I kept knocking it open. So you must have seen it at least twice, the burn on my knuckle: once when it was raw, and next when it was better. When we are together, you often take my fingers and press them to your mouth. But now I have a burn you have not seen, and it is almost healed. It did not hurt very much the first or the second day. It turned a darker red, the color of a wine stain, but on the third night it began to burn.

It kept me up, a night visitor. But one I had invited myself, as I invite so many things.

The burn turned a darker red, the color of a port-wine stain. When I was little, I had a birthmark on my right shoulder blade, a large splotch. Between the ages of nine and thirteen I wore a shirt on the beach because I was embarrassed. Then I forgot about it. Now the marks are gone, replaced by others. It didn't occur to me that other girls had their own catalog of flaws: to me they seemed unmarked and unencumbered. Pom asked, the other day, whether I knew that in French *ouch* is not *ouch* but *aïe*. What is it in Italian? she asked. You must ask Lorenzo. You tell me a story about burns: After an affair with a Belgian woman, you did not see her for ten years, and then she called you in the middle of the night. She was in the hospital. In her house in France, in the country, she had fallen in front of a fireplace. Her stockings caught fire. She had been burned over forty percent of her body. You remembered that exactly: forty percent. A terrible thing. You saw her again, after that. Well, this is not that, I said. A deflection: what is there to complain about, really? A little patch of sunlight? Are you thinking of lying down in it?

The burn was covered by the dress I bought yesterday, which I chose because the silk is printed with swirls, like the marbleized paper that once upon a time you could only buy at Il Papiro in Florence, but now, like everything else, you can get it anywhere. This morning the burned skin is sandpaper, the skin bunching a little, as when you catch a thread in a sweater and the weave puckers. It is still burning. The household, which consists at the moment of Pom and Frank, here for a week, is exasperated by my lack of interest in it—what lack of interest, you would say, reading this, all you do is carry on about this so-called burn. They are proponents of aloe and ice. I think it is just one more hurt I am doing nothing about. And I can hear you saying, it is inelegant to feel sorry for yourself, *cara*, and not what I would expect of you, who can make a fire with one stick in the forest. Did you learn that in the Girl Scouts? I was not a Girl Scout, I was a Brownie, for about two weeks. But, you say, you are a Girl Scout now—*un'Esploratrice*. You have to be grown-up, *cara mia*, to be a Girl Scout.

On Friday when I learned the word for owl in Spanish, the class also taught me the rules of manhunt, which is exactly like tag and hide-and-seek played at the same time. The best places are parking lots and fire escapes. I did not play manhunt. They all played it. It does not have a beautiful name, like *nascondino*, *cache-cache*, or hide-and-seek, which has in its name the idea that if you hide, someone will come and find you. This morning the burn has only one small strip of brown skin clinging to it, but in the bath, it turns red, the blood beneath objecting to anything that reminds it of heat. I recount to you my imperfections: the wen on the back of my right knee, the knot of veins on the inside of my left thigh that often aches, and is prominent now if I stand bare legs together. The map of capillaries on my left ankle. The very small scars on my left breast. A chicken-pox scar on my forehead. The vestigial nipple under my right breast. You have not noted a single one of these. When I went to see Alastair, that was what he liked, those marks.

When Michael Rockefeller disappeared, his dugout canoe turned over in the river, and the brown water rushed over him.

He thought he could make it, swimming the three miles to shore. The boat drifted. René Wassing, who waited in the boat for help, paddling among the snakes and the leeches, survived. Anything is possible. A girl can fall out of an airplane which has been hit by lightning, and be cradled by the branches of a tree two miles below. A girl who loved butterflies. In the gallery, on the Bis poles, which commemorate the dead, a canoe is often carved halfway up the trunk, or halfway down, so that the spirit of the dead can row to the next world. A fairy tale. The other day, when Frank and I were waiting for a movie to start—I don't remember which movie it was; when he and I are together we go to a lot of movies, as the stage of staying in bed is over, or perhaps impossible, since the places we find ourselves are always full of cats and children; you are more anxious about Esther and the plumbers. But I was telling you a story about Frank—we do not speak about him as a rule, as the rule is we take the furnishings of each other's lives for granted, but here is a story he told me about an afternoon when he was quite small. He was playing catch with a round rubber ball. Part of the game was that there was a tub of water between the players—he and another little boy. After you threw the ball, you jumped over the tub of water and changed places. But the point of the story is that when he jumped over the water, he heard his father's voice speaking to him, as though his father was there in the yard, rather than a few miles away on the other side of town. A man who smoked too much, who looked like a movie star. He played ball for three minor-league teams: baseball, basketball, and football. But that afternoon Frank was playing catch. I think they'd played for a while before they decided to incorporate the tub of water into the game. It was May, but cold and gray. The water was cold when it splashed. His mother was there, and she chided them for playing with the water.

When he jumped, he heard his father's voice, calling him. At first, he dismissed it. His father was at home, it was a Saturday. But when it happened a third time, he stopped playing and said to his mother that they had to go home. Because his mother was born in Trieste and her own mother had second sight, they got into the car at once, without her handbag. His mother had to go back into the house to get it, a big alligator bag with a tarnished clasp, while Frank waited for her in the passenger seat, where a piece of the burgundy Naugahyde was peeling, and he sat and teased it. This part he did not tell me, but I can see the bag and feel under my own hand the satisfaction of the Naugahyde pulling away. When they got home, his father was lying on the steps to the cellar where he had fallen. When Frank tells this story, he is careful to say that he heard his father's voice calling him only when he jumped over the water.

The sink in your bathroom does not work, and you need to have the floor fixed before you put it back. In this house, the toilets need to be replaced. My father has sent me a check for the toilets—he is a believer in modern sanitation, but his superstitions operate here, too: he will not drink water from the bathroom tap. The check is exactly one third of what the new toilets will cost. But perhaps some things need to remain awry, so the real disasters can remain hidden. When I left today, in a voice that is unusual for you, gruff, you said you do not like to wash after I leave. And I said, as if this odd life of ours will continue, we will remember this as the year you had no sink. One day driving with the children on a cloverleaf that spun us off to a residential street on the way out to Long Island, I realized I was lost. We found our way back, but I said, to reassure them, I know I'm lost but I've been lost here before.

And we laughed, all of us, in the car. That's it, Satchmo. I've been lost before.

A widening gyre. The past basted with a blanket stitch, the devil's tiny pitchfork. I return again to the first time—I was running late to pick up Pom at school, and I looked at my watch before I stepped on to the bus. It was exactly 3:18. It is my grandmother's watch, and the numbers are quite small, so I had to squint to see the placement of the hands. But I did not get on the bus—we waited at the bus stop and the bus did not come, and you hailed a cab and put me into it. And you told the driver the name and address of the school; only when the taxi left the curb did I think: how odd, that you would know that, the name of her school and the address. I ask you about it now, months later, in the restaurant where we sit at the table by the window having lunch. It is warm; in a flash it will be summer. I am thinking that one day I will learn to live without the sound that you make in the back of your throat, that difficult h. A small thing. (And so what, I can hear you say, so what? And then?) You order for me in the restaurant: she will have ——. Only you do this. My grandfather did this: my granddaughter will have the chocolate sundae. What is it that I will have? Of course, you say, you knew the name of the school.

You are telling me about a telephone call. A woman called, from Boca Raton. From Sacramento. From the world of the lost. From Mars. An old woman. As she spoke, you realized she was describing the *fattoria* and grounds that belonged to your grandmother's sister, Ludmilla. You did not see Ludmilla often because your grandmother, who had six sisters, did not speak to her, but you remember the house well, and the garden. You say now, I said to her, I can see the door where the soldiers took the children, and where they knocked. The woman was silent on the phone, and you could tell that she did not want to talk but did not want to hang up either. A friend of a friend had said, he might remember. The garden and the lizard on the wall, the cans of pork, the nuns, the father taken away in a car. The nuns took the children. She wants to know what happened to the mother. We know what happened to the mother, you told her.

Yes, you said to me, we know what happened to the mother. But she was not well, there was something the matter with her. And the daughter hopes she died in transit? I asked. Yes, that is what she hopes. But it will be possible to find out. That is the thing about the Germans. At least in Italy it will be possible to find out. We are sitting in a restaurant that we have each gone to how many times, separately and together, a few blocks from your apartment. I was here three days ago, at Easter, with the children. Your hand is over mine. In restaurants and cafés and coffee shops you have a habit of turning your head and looking into space. The first few times this happened, my heart stopped, and at once I felt irritated at myself. What is he to you? I said to myself, sternly. It is a way you show me that you can withdraw your attention. Inside the restaurant it is brightly lit. The waitress is too attentive. I am busy as a bee, shredding my bread into tiny pieces and playing with the sugar canister, which looks like a medieval helmet; it opens and shuts with a snap. I am picturing the mother in a brown dress in the back of a wagon. I do not know why it is a wagon rather than a train car, or why she is alone in the wagon, like a cow going to market, a wagon that looks like an oxcart in an illustrated book of old-fashioned tales. I used to think that I could not think about these things because I was so sensitive; I could imagine them too clearly, more sensitively than other people could imagine them, and because of this supposed extreme sensitivity, I thought that the pitch of horror was a pitch that I could hear better than others, like a sound that can only be heard by snakes or dogs. This exempted me, I thought, my extreme sensitivity. But the truth was I didn't want to think about it. Can we, as Pom says, *can we just*? Later, in bed, I took your hand and placed it over my mouth, a starfish, an oxygen mask. What is the story in which the lost girl breathes from an upturned flower? Make me not a rebuke to the foolish. Did you have any idea? I asked. When I was leaving your apartment, you kept one hand on my waist as I put on my boots. Your dream is to keep me prisoner, a dream in which I collude.

A long time ago when you lived in Montalcino, you had a greyhound named Bell. As a puppy he had been tortured. When he ran on the dog track he was very fast, but when he got too far ahead of the other dogs, he would stop and wait for them to catch up. When he came back from the track, he was beaten, but he did not know why he was being beaten; too much time had elapsed after his transgression. But how could he have known? He flinched when he saw his owner. This man had two young greyhounds, and you bought Bell from him. And that was that? I asked. Yes, that was that. So while the last thing in the world you wanted was a dog, you had a dog. Many of your stories are about this, how you acquired the last thing you wanted. After many other things? Not the best for last, but here it is, *at last*. The *and, or, not* of Boolean logic. One thing leading to another. In Montalcino you were living with some artists and actors in a loft over a farmhouse. The farmer was convinced Bell was going to eat his chickens. Whether or not he would eat the chickens, he chased them. The farmer put ground glass in his food.

In Boston the last stop on the Blue Line is Wonderland—once when I was in school, I went with some friends to see the dog races. It may be that I have made it up—going to the dog races. I can smell the stench of the track, and hear the high-pitched keening of the dogs, feel the trash under my feet. My hands are over my eyes. But that does not mean we did go—only that I thought of going so often, it is as if we had gone. Did I or did I not go to the dog races? The woman in the brown dress is taken away in 1943 in a cart, she is too ill to throw herself against the sides of the cart, to try to climb out. Instead, she stands still. Her eyes are shut and there is no place to sit down—it is packed with people, some of whom have lost control of their bowels; the sky is blue, carrion birds are flying in circles above the cart. She is swaying. I did not think about this because I didn't want to think about it. No more or less than anyone else.

What does that mean, *long enough*? you asked. I had said, this has gone on long enough. How do you know? you asked. *Let's play monster.* Here is some more of the story. The woman on the phone had only a very few memories, before she lived with her sisters, of Ludmilla. After all, she was seven. Or eight. Her strongest memory was of a funeral for cousins of her mother who had been murdered. This was 1937, or '38. When I look it up, the story comes together in one high-pitched whistle: two brothers, antifascists, shot dead by the Cagoulards. I did not go to the dog races. This morning I told you about a friend who was attacked in his apartment, in Philadelphia. How did you find out? you asked. Because to you and me, that is always part of the story—how it is told to you. Along a telephone wire that is no longer a wire but a radio wave, electrical signals turned into a string of numbers. When I think of that time now, the months we spent together, until time pulled apart, like an accordion or, better, a Japanese fan, torn in spots, but still printed with a panorama which I refused to see: the smoking volcano, the deep river, the cart going downhill—a series of disasters, the Sèvres cup whizzing by your head, death by water and death by fire, other moments small and indistinguishable. But those were perhaps the most important. Because they became ordinary, our life as it was.

This morning Pom looked at my arm, where there is now another burn, a two-part scorch mark above the old fading one, nearer my wrist, and said, Mommy, you must be careful. There is nothing like eliding the truth to open a chasm. And then as it widens, you begin to shout things over it, reasons and explanations, none of which have to do with anything but that you are shouting. I left my hat at the restaurant, and you went to get it the next morning. Is this what we do now, you write to me at dawn, leave our belongings in restaurants? Last night, you told me another story.

For a few months, you are living in Belgium. By some coincidence or other, in this little town, Nina Simone is staying at a small hotel. But is this right? In 1988 she moves to Nijmegen, near Amsterdam. I cannot find a reference to any stay of any length in Belgium after 1980, for it would had to have been then—because before that you were too young; she was here, not there. In the nineties, when this is more probable, this meeting of yours, she lived in France, at Carry-le-Rouet, near Aix-en-Provence. She recorded "Baltimore" in 1978.

> *Get my sister Sandy*
> *And my little brother Ray*
> *Buy a big old wagon*
> *To haul us all away*

In Belgium, you said, you found the hotel where she was staying and called her room. She was there to avoid the press, she was in a terrible state, tired and ill. What made you think that she would want to see you? Who can tell what leads us to the things of this world? In any case she came downstairs, the nimbus around her glittering despite a face the color of ash. Come back at four, she said. We'll go for a drive. It was a gray day—it is always gray in Belgium. But in your story, it is a few years earlier, and you are in the hotel, waiting for Nina Simone to come downstairs in the elevator, which stops for an age at each floor. Its walls are made of fake wood, not green leather. She must operate it herself, which means remembering which buttons to push. When Louie was very little, we lived in a building with an elevator, on the fourth floor—and she learned to press 4. *Sailboat, sailboat*, she sang, her thumb reaching up for the button.

It is always raining in Belgium. I remember being there for a day or two twenty years ago; it seemed to be raining inside the train car. Where was I going? I think I flew into Brussels and took a train to Paris—then, one never went directly anywhere, there was plenty of time for money-saving detours, to visit a friend who might be living in Nantes, in Liège, in Aix, studying French film. I remember the course my friend was taking; a French class, in which the only text was the film *Jules et Jim*. By the end of the summer she spoke French beautifully, but her vocabulary was limited; as in a triangle, which at first seems to multiply possibilities but instead reduces them: *Le bonheur n'est pas facile à dire et s'use sans que personne ne s'en aperçoive*; the rotten rose ripped from the wall; a triangle hit with a tiny hammer, the sound of the cash register ringing up a sale. To find our friend we walked through the lavender laden with bees, and even then I knew, *Remember this.*

She came down in pale fur. Let's go for a drive, she said. She had a car, and a driver. It was a long car, like a hearse, a 1956 Impala. What was such a car doing in Belgium in 1985? Who knows? It might as well have been driven by a team of mice. The wide back seat of the car was red leather. Because it was Belgium, it felt as if it was raining in the car, eddies of water like Florentine endpapers—Just say it was raining, I hear you say. Her lipstick was orange. All about her were little bits of frost, on her hair, her skin, as if she had been gilded.

For you, there are two kinds of stories: one in which someone knocks on your door, or calls from the street or a distant city, or waits in the doorway across from your window, to catch your attention, which snags on whatever comes near, a child or a pet, neither of which holds your attention very long, and discovers, despite how it seems, your rapt regard is at best whimsical and a precursor of loss, a mourning dove. Because everything for you is a love affair, which by its nature ends with a limp. In the other story you knock on a door. Inside the house, or the tower or the hotel, with its waist-high maze, is a very old person—an old poet, or a *baronessa,* or an orphan, whom you want to come out of hiding, someone who with your urging will do a little dance or sing a song. You have gone to see them, out of pity or grief or something else, whatever it is you go to see people for, to find the lost piece of a puzzle they have kept in their pocket, among the lint and the old coins, Indian head nickels, Cray-Pas—my grandfather drew with Cray-Pas, I remember, typing that word, the pastels got all over his clothes and mine when I was with him, streaks of yellow on the navy serge—that will help you put yourself back if not together, to add to the debris in the pocket of your blue jacket, the one you have been wearing that is a little too heavy for the warmer weather we have been having these past few days as summer approaches.

But who is the mourning dove? In Aesop's story, a thirsty ant goes down to the wild river. The ant will drown, but a dove on an overhanging branch lets a leaf fall into the current—the ant climbs onto the barge of the leaf and is saved. Soon, a bird catcher comes to trap the dove, setting his snare of lime twigs. The ant bites him on the foot; the hunter's cry of pain startles the dove, who flies off to safety.

> I saw the dove come down, the dove with the green twig, the childish dove out of the storm and flood. It came toward me in the style of the Holy Spirit descending. I had been sitting in a café for twenty-five years waiting for this vision. It hovered over the great quarrel. I surrendered to the iron laws of the moral universe which make a boredom out of everything desired. Do not surrender, said the dove. I have come to make a nest in your shoe. I want your step to be light.

Who is in peril, and who is saved? Sometimes I feel that you have towed me to safety; perhaps we do not get to choose where we feel safe. On July 29, 1961, his college sweetheart, Patsy Lane Cushman, wrote to Michael Rockefeller, "The word for this week is *inscrutable*." The pale blue air letter a little creased. The catamaran began to take on water. In the leaves of the boxwood hedge, a little stereopticon of dew, each one a reflection of a tiny swimmer. I am always late when I come to meet you, but I am also too early. Much later I would love someone with whom I imagined a past: with you I only imagine the future. I do not think, what if we had met then, in the elevator on Park Avenue? We were sixteen, seventeen. A different world. You say, if you do not trust me, if you cannot let go, there is nothing—do you really think I would forget you after two weeks? And if I did, what would you want me for? My whole life is about remembering. You are very hard on me. You always say that. I say that because it is true.

As I type this morning, the phone rings three times: my father, you, and Frank, who calls every morning. When I was a child, I had a toy box telephone, painted blue. One afternoon when I was bored, waiting for a friend to come and play, my mother said, find something to do. I lifted up the little red receiver. At that very moment, the doorbell rang. What is the shortest distance between two points? Between grief and delight? I slept late this morning because Pom is at a friend's, on the other side of the park. I was going to see you, but—you text in the afternoon, while I am on the bus—Valeria has a kidney infection and, you tell me, Esther brought her to your apartment where she is in the guest-room bed. A courtly gesture, to let me know she was not in your bed. But of course, Esther would not put her in your bed. It is Esther, who thinks of Valeria as a friend, who is the dupe, as she makes up the guest-room bed—which I might add has a working sink in the adjacent bathroom! You text me about this, and then call and tell me twice. Valeria's husband seems to reside nowhere, not even at the end of a telephone. (Maybe it is not true, maybe she does not have a husband or children in Prague or in Slovakia, perhaps she is married to you?) If the picture of Valeria that I have found on the Internet is of the correct person, she does not look well. The look of a toxin under her skin, a woman, as you tell me this morning, who has only one kidney. But there is no child tearing up magazines in your apartment the color of the inside of a shell, is there? *Un po' troppo, tutto questo, no?* Perhaps it is different for others, the solutions they come up with, though it is peculiarly un-American, the distrust of hospitals—better to die at home on your own sheets from Pratesi, waited on by someone who is growing sick of you or, if you allow yourself to be taken to your lover's apartment by his girlfriend, who does not know that she is sharing her lover with not one but two people. I am not saying that person could not be me—in the waters off beautiful Nauset, every woman adores a fascist—but at the moment it is not. A detail: she is sleeping in the guest room. A backhanded compliment, as if it matters, a kind of splitting of hairs. But I can't complain about that now. Before going home I went to the market—we are out of milk and eggs. Now when George and Louie are home they look in the icebox and say accusingly, how long has this been here? How long has anything been here? Too long.

But what kind of stories do I tell? Stories about people who lose their way when they are telling stories, who can't tell a hawk from a handsaw. Now, it is six o'clock in the morning and I am up, typing, in the whir of the old air conditioner. May, but already hot. In California, wildfires. My stories are tales of perpetual half-lives, the pages strewn across the long dining room, fluttering along the table, the heart elsewhere because it is safe nowhere. In class last week: *the drama of endangerment is the trope of writing about the environment.* But that is the trope of every story. That afternoon in my office where through the open window we could hear the bells—cowbells, according to Sam, who came by after the end of my midday seminar. I said, you do not want to get to the point where the license plate on the car ahead of you is sending you a secret message. But how do I stop that from happening? he asked. Sam has dyed a blue streak in his hair, and has been shaving so closely he looks about twelve years old and skinned. It's a long conversation, I said. He brought me a print of four ice-cream cones, with the handwritten legend: *If you go for this?* The night of Pablo's party, you brought me a ridiculous bouquet of flowers, too tall for any vase, calla lilies and gigantic primroses: it is the adage, I guess, of hiding something in plain sight. Something even I didn't see then. What was the phrase George used at dinner the other night? "Plausible deniability."

On Friday afternoon when I went to meet you at the movies, I realized when I got off at West Fourth Street that I had forgotten to put on my earrings. On Bleecker Street in front of Our Lady of Pompeii—a street fair, and a Greek woman selling earrings, all ten dollars. A pair of gold-plated knots. She said, "I cannot go out without three things: my perfume, my lipstick, and earrings. I would not be myself!" Who would she be, I wondered? A complicit glance. She was perhaps sixty, with platinum hair, wearing a zipped-up black-and-white anorak. Five minutes later I was wearing the gold knots when I met you on Carmine Street, at the little coffee shop. I had an Americano and you an espresso, and then we left to walk to Film Forum. Why did you write FF on the paper? you asked. Because I carry too many scraps of paper and to remind me that this is the confirmation number at Film Forum. Where do you want to sit? Not behind the pole. In the next row a woman was talking to a man who looked like her son but turned out to be her husband. She was reprimanding herself for nagging him about a lamp that needed to be rewired, and while chiding herself for nagging, continued to nag him. She talked until the film credits began and through the previews, which included a film about Hannah Arendt. At a state dinner Harold Macmillan asked Arendt what she was looking forward to in retirement, and she said, a penis. She meant happiness.

The clinic now closed, Valeria back in Prague, or on Pluto, you respond with three emails in five minutes and call twice. A therapy session with Victor yesterday morning which I record here. It was so hot that my blouse was sticking to my back by the time I climbed the fetid stairs, too hot for this time of year. Victor says neurotic behavior is a hypnagogic state, or the symptom of one: the mind is given a suggestion and then repeats its response again and again. I told him that I wondered whether I was addicted to anxiety, that my reflexive action—of missing you, of the inaccessibility of the loved one, the feeling of absence that my heart enjoins by shutting down, and then beating its wings against the cage it has made—was what I was after, rather than you yourself. I'm in the import-export business, said Victor. What can that mean? I have been studying how I may compare this prison where I live unto the world. I am thinking of all the things, *il mio caro*, I do not tell you and perhaps never will. The story bites its own tail. I am meeting you at eleven a.m. and then getting the car and driving the girls to the country to Alida's for the long weekend, so must pack. I love you, you said, on the phone yesterday as I was making supper. What can that possibly mean? It is going to be ninety-two degrees today. Your email: Just to confirm, see you at 11 at my place.

Years ago—I was in my twenties—when I was living in Assisi for a short time, there was a woman who walked up and down a stretch of road that led up to Santa Maria di Lignano.

She walked every day, in every weather, maybe two miles up and the same distance down. It was spring, and yellow *ginestra* lined the road. She was a young woman, perhaps my age then, twenty-six or twenty-seven, with short black greasy hair parted and held with a barrette. She wore some kind of light pants and a white shirt. Sometimes, a sweater tied around her waist. She had a limp, so that walking was slipshod and difficult. The road had no shoulder. When a car skidded around a curve, she plastered herself to the slight embankment of gravel and the dense hedge. She breathed heavily through her mouth. Once I decided to walk up to the village from the shrine to Sant'Agata because I wanted to pass her, to see her up close. She had waxy, clear white skin, slightly shiny with sweat, exophthalmic brown eyes, and scabs of eczema or psoriasis on her lids. Her neck was dirty, and her collarbone exposed by the open collar of her shirt was delicate, scapular.

The woman who walked up and down the hill to Santa Maria di Lignano, what did she want up there? I found out later there had been a birth injury; the prescription was to walk up and down every day. How things can go wrong with so little provocation. As I type this morning I can feel the hollow pain in my hip, which returns when I am ill or distressed. It started one night at the theater; I tore the muscle turning the heel of my boot in the interval. The play was *Heartbreak House*. In the final act, a tremendous crash. "The next one will get us," says Captain Shotover. Mrs. Hushabye: "Did you hear the explosions? And the sound in the sky: it's splendid: it's like an orchestra: it's like Beethoven!" Beethoven, who could only hear the music in his head, like Richard at Pomfret Castle. The hobbyhorse takes the jump, released from its iron trestle, the nick on its bottom showing as it sails over the gate. How the past catches us up, whinnying its fanfares, its complaints. The woman who walked up and down the hill, what did she want up there? Some things do not change, you said. But you are wrong. Voices outside, garbage trucks, the day beginning.

At last an inkling, which is what it is, a small, inked-in figure seen through the opera glasses from the fourth ring, the beset child hurrying from one side of the paper to another, trying to keep it level, a paddle her only lever. Do you remember how beautiful the light was on the Boat Pond, the dinghies shifting the shining water as we watched from the bench, and the French schoolchildren passed, nattering under the trees, the leaves rippling the spring sky, the cloud rafts circling to pick up the drowned. I am reading *The Ambassadors*. Strether says of Maria Gostrey, "She was surely not to break away at the very moment she had created a want." That page brittle, about to fall out: "Everything he wanted was comprised moreover in a single boon—the common unattainable art of taking things as they came . . . Oh if he *should* do the sum no slate would hold the figures!" But which one of them is you?

*A bubble wand. On the desk, a vase of dried cornflowers, another of dried bark peeled from a sycamore, a whelk egg case, also dried, a balsa-wood model like a little boat, a painted fan, a green enamel paperweight in the shape of a pear. No. Step back. Not yet. The future still bound up tight.*

Tiny bubbles of rainbow dew on the boxwood. Squint. Three hundred years ago, a goshawk, sun bright on its dun feathers, marks the furred line of trees along the east flank of Lomse Island, the stony bank of Kneiphof Island, and the small church tower with its topaz *star. Prussia. And across the Pregel River, the turrets of Königsberg Castle; beyond it, the peninsula, near where on the painted map boats with square sails are veering toward the harbor. A local game: the seven city bridges—if wishing made it so, you could circle the city, crossing one bridge after another and end up where you started. But no. Leonhard Euler, who as a child spent Saturday afternoons learning mathematics with Bernouli's younger brother, "who was gracious enough to comment on the collected difficulties," proved that given these seven bridges, you can only retrace your steps. Forward. Back. The beginning of graph theory. A maze is not a labyrinth. A century's pressure like a flower press: one thought atop another, a palimpsest. Caroline at four in the boxwood. Press the keys: Cork, in 1854, white swans passing under the leaded windows of High Bridge, the vermilion leaves of the beech tree. Mary Everest, who married the mathematician George Boole, said, "At seventeen, a thought struck him suddenly, which became the foundation of all his future discoveries. It was a flash of psychological insight into the conditions under which a mind most readily accumulates knowledge: No general method for the solution of questions in the theory of probabilities can be established which does not explicitly recognise, not only the special numerical bases of the science, but also those universal laws of thought which are the basis of all reasoning." His paper on the universe of discourse proved that one thing leads to another until it doesn't. A row of toppled pins:* And, Or, Not. *Stop. Reset. Beyond the boxwood, a series of iron hoops mark the edge of the azalea hedge, the bee circling until it stings:* I won't, I won't. I won't go with you, I want to stay with Grandpa! *Foot stamp.* Wait here, *said her aunt. A shadow in the boxwood hedge. Press again. A handprint like a starfish. By 1912, the Aeolian Company had nine thousand rolls on order for its player piano, including "Hello! Ma Baby." "I'se got a little baby but she's outta sight / I talk to her across the telephone / I'se never seen my honey, but she's mine, alright." Sing, says the thinking heart, ear cocked to the receiver. A girl who would grow up to wait for a telephone call, to read the tea leaves of a time stamp. She shuts her eyes tight. What the eye doesn't see. When I'm calling you, will you answer, too?*

*One war, then another. In 1942, in Königsberg, at Tommerholzplatz: book burning in the square, the burnt pages with no choice but to let the singed letters go, charred, red-hot above the bonfire, their loops and edges buckling, trying to hold on to the thoughts that had made them billow and sing—someone reading, up late, the lamp lit—those black bits loosed in air and turned to crows rising over the river, the ratcheting caw of their alarm call, their wings blackened pages. Sun up, sun down. A stone's throw away, in the cipher room, the German army sent morning messages by radio. The girls at Bletchley Park called it catching fish. The word fish a verb with a hook in its mouth. What the eye doesn't see, the heart doesn't grieve over. Minnows over the river rocks, the willows springing up along the watercourse. In 1948, Claude Shannon, in "A Mathematical Theory of Communication": the channel is "merely the medium used to transmit the signal from transmitter to receiver." A year later, in Princeton, for Christmas, his wife Betty gave him a Meccano set. By Easter, he tried, first, a mechanized turtle; next, a mouse, called Theseus, with wire whiskers, set down in a Meccano maze that measured twenty-six inches by twenty-eight. The mouse sniffed the air. "When Theseus encounters an obstacle he rotates in a circular manner until he finds a means of escape. He also keeps in mind the direction from which he entered the square." It was Ariadne, the Minotaur's sister, who gave Theseus the thread. Every iota of information peeled down to its smallest bit, so that the mouse, traversing the maze's hidden electric grid, learned from experience—experience sorted out, like a hand of playing cards; diamonds, hearts. Let me call you sweetheart. At Bell Labs, Shannon picked up the telephone: "Information is not what you do say but what you could say." What's the shortest distance between two points? Two tin cans and a wire. But* it's not the length of the wire but what the wire intersects. Shannon said, "Communications and cryptography were so close together you couldn't separate them." Hush. Heard but not seen, seen but not heard. Ssh. Operator please. Don't pull it. A dropped stitch in the smocking. A child with her mouth stitched tight.

A child in a white smocked dress, in the boxwood, butting her huge head. At twelve, Ada Lovelace, who drew an enormous pair of wings to help a horse to fly, wrote to her friend Woronozow Grieg, the son of her tutor Mary Somerville, that she desired to construct a calculus that would measure the sensibilities of the nervous system. How does the brain give rise to thoughts and the nerves to feelings? Press the keys. Who is he when he's at home? It's Greek, from the Greek. "The great art of life is sensation," wrote her father, Lord Byron. Uh-oh. Press the keys. What does Caroline hear? Her father singing. He said, Miss Mouse will you marry me, uh-huh? One, zero. "You say you love and yet your eye / No symptom of that love conveys." What will the wedding supper be? Nine pins: And, Or, Not. Again. One. Zero. Next to come in was the bumblebee, uh-huh. Press the keys. Why should we shrink from what we cannot shun? You are my sunshine, my only sunshine. It is important to stand very still, singing to herself in the boxwood. The bees make a humming sound. In Köningsberg, the hawk a fighter jet, a black iris over the river and the islands, the small voles in the weeds, the glittering flies. Pie in the sky. Gone, the river's narrative, the transmigration of souls. In Princeton, Alan Turing and Claude Shannon, heads bowed together over the same maze box. Even the iris coded now, the goshawk's gaze a fingerprint. Drink to me only with thine eyes. Has anyone ever told you? Yes. She shifts from foot to foot. Written inside her shoe the letter A, for Aster, a flower named for a star. A bee in the calyx. C is for Caroline. Jeepers, creepers, where'd you get those peepers? Bright star, the moving waters at their priestlike task. The boxwood's furry cat smell. Oh dear, oh dear, I shall be late!

*Call me when you get there. Water dripping. A thread loose in the smocking. Don't tug it. Press the keys. If you want any more you can sing it yourself. A girl in the leaves. I went from love to loss by way of lose. Hurry up, it's time! How long? Tick-tock went the crocodile clock. The sun shall not smite thee by day nor the moon by night. A red can floating in the channel. It doesn't make no nevermind. What's next? An ear to the ground. Baci, baci, baci. How many times do I have to tell you? Bird on a wire. Don't sit under the apple tree with anyone else but me, no, no, no, anyone else but me.* And, Or, Not. *Letters curl and char above her head. Answer me, missy. Skywriting. What does the little bird say? C is for Caroline. Cuckoo, cuckoo. I see you. No time. In the boxwood hedge, a mouse with a pink tail, she stands stock-still in her white smocked dress, listening.*

In the top drawer in your bedroom, your cuff links and your mother's amethyst ring, in velvet pouches inside a wooden box. A reliquary. When I was first married, we had a small boat. At the yard where we bought it, every boat was made of wood; the boat was like that, a little reliquary, holding an insane notion: to keep such a boat. The woodwork was polished with beeswax. We moored the boat in the cove, and kept the dinghy on Cormorant Neck, in a crescent of upturned boats past the shipwreck I had walked to every day as a child. A small girl, so brave, allowed to cross the sandy road, through a hedge of broom, on her way to a shipwreck. We sold it; it was too expensive for either of us to keep. The other day, on the radio, a composer was talking about a passage in a ballet score for piano and viola, and how in that section the beat or melody of the two instruments will not and does not match. One note, he said, was his father, and the other his mother. One steady and the other—circling. When I was a child and went sailing every day in the summer with my father, he taught me to tack by taking me out in open water and throwing a life preserver overboard. I had to circle the life preserver twice, then stop and pick it up. Because I was an imaginative child, a circumstance I would wish on no one, each time I felt without question that I was saving someone from drowning. And then beneath that fear was the terror that I would be left to drown. I would have to save myself, I knew. It was no one else's job, to pluck the life preserver from the water. The boat was called the *Nausicaa*. And my brother, three years younger, at the tiller. As a child one learns about coercion. James thinks, Cam thinks, in the boat headed to the lighthouse, in the wake of grief, "But their father, they knew, would never be content until they were flying along . . . He had made them come. He had forced them to come. In their anger they hoped that the breeze would never rise, that he might be thwarted in every possible way, since he had forced them to come against their wills." You asked, a few months ago when we were driving back from Long Island, what was the beginning of the claustrophobia? The feeling of being trapped in a small boat in open water. Nausicaa rescuing Odysseus when he appears naked in the woods, a secret.

Somewhere there is a set of contact sheets of this shipwreck, like a huge gray bird. Now it has fallen to pieces. We took photographs, Alastair and I, I think, for two years. I was perhaps twenty-two; he was twenty-four. It was a time before we had seen many things fall apart, and the idea of it intrigued us—now the last thing we want is more evidence of the world collapsing in on itself, in fire, wind, and water—it will not be until decades later that the desire stirs again, when ruin is what there is left of so many loved things. A hundred years after my own childhood, it was the first place my children were allowed to walk alone.

They collected nails from the sand; old, rusted, ancient nails that held nothing together. The children liked to walk to it in any kind of weather, and why not? Once they'd exhausted the shelves of ghost stories and fairy tales, there was so little to do in the house. Michael, row the boat ashore, I sang to them. What happened to Michael's boat? Was it towed ashore? Recovered from the village, Michael's New Guinea notebooks are stained with damp, the blue ink marbleizing the page, where he reproduced by hand the beautiful geometric and swirling patterns characteristic of Asmat designs. From the search log:

> From The Hellwig River south to Frederic Henrik Island was the area of the search. Between Eilandan River and Pirmapoem, where the boat reportedly capsized, and then, from there, about five miles north. From here the search was continued for about 25–50 along the shore. Every day the area was searched by planes, ships, small boats, and helicopters.

There are some things there is no help for. The other morning when I left you asleep and then returned to bed, you said, I do not know how you do it, for me the morning is full of ghosts. How do I do it? This is how—an answer so obvious and banal, my impulse is to delete it. When you got up, you put on a black-and-white-striped bathrobe I had not seen before. You said, my father had a bathrobe exactly like this and for months he wore it and did not come out of his room. Where did you find it? I asked. I bought it on Madison Avenue.

Your father had a bathrobe exactly like this one, and for months he wore it and did not come out of his room. The telephone rang. You were fourteen. Your mother, you said, had taken you on a vacation to Bermuda. Your father had not come along, but this wasn't unusual. When you returned, you did not go home; she took you and Susanna to a different house, on the road that goes up from Siena to Monteriggioni, a small dirt road off that road. Do you know that road? Yes. Not the small dirt road. Graziella, the housekeeper, was there. With the dog? No, that dog had died. The telephone rang. Who found him? Passersby. Passersby? He was in a car. On May 24, 1975, your father took an overdose of tranquilizers in his car, in Rome, on a small side street near the Flaminia. Or was it 1976? The night he died you went to a party given by an older cousin. You took Susanna's Vespa, although you were not yet allowed to ride a Vespa at night. What right do I have to write this down? No right. You took the Vespa. Your cousin was a few years older—seventeen or eighteen. You wandered around the party. In the middle of the party—you said there was a lot of commotion, but it was quiet in the trees. I sat with a girl that I knew, a little bit, in the branches. It was nice. The girl was wearing a white dress, and I kissed her a little—this and that, no more—and I talked to her. You were fourteen. Yes, I was fourteen. We talked together, and then she began to talk, and I listened. I have no memory at all of what she said. Of course not, I said, you don't listen. I saw her a little, later. And then it got dark and I went home. There is part of a story that I have forgotten, some trouble getting home, lost on the winding, leaf-strewn roads. It was very late. That is your story? I asked. Yes. I said, it is the story you always tell: a girl, a wood, and a white dress. This is entirely different! The story of arriving too young on a Vespa. And that you left a different person than the boy you had been yesterday. It is the anniversary of his death, tomorrow. No one in the family spoke to my mother; they blamed her for leaving him. Did you blame her? No. The girl was the age Pom is now.

Now it is a week later, we were in the shower, and you were soaping my back and you said, I should have been warmer, with Stefano. The next morning, an email. You had a nightmare, and then got up early, in a sweat, looking for me. You imagined that I was in the kitchen wearing the black-and-white robe.

One thing that happens when I arrive at your apartment—first, when I'm downstairs and buzz up, there is a small moment when I wonder if you are there, and if you will answer; I fix my hair in the lobby mirror. If you do not answer, that would be your way of saying no. I know you would not do it—for one thing your manners are too good—but it is there, that fear. When you buzz back, there's a lag between the first door and the second door to the lobby, and I do a certain amount of futile pulling until you buzz again. You have lived in this apartment off and on I think for twenty-five years. The décor of the lobby is like a hundred others, the combination of grandeur—marble and mirrors—and grime that characterizes buildings on the Upper West Side. When I was a child I avoided mirrors. As I type I find myself thinking of how other women on their way up to your apartment have fixed their hair in the mirror. When I was on my way over, you called and asked where I was. I said on Broadway, and I could tell from your voice that you expected me to be in the vestibule, when instead I was on Ninetieth Street, picking up my watch at the jeweler, who once again had jostled the battery to make it tick.

I know there are other visitors—there is no sense in looking for proof except for the need to press on a cut. How long? Long enough. When I arrived upstairs, you answered the door in bare feet. There is rarely proof. Last night a dish of pistachios and an unopened bar of expensive chocolate. A little narrative. But here, I do not even bother to put a question mark. A little clue. For whom? Because, after all, this "thing I am writing I don't know what it is, etc.," is a letter for you. And you do not need clues. Are you hungry? you ask. I have eaten one piece of toast since this morning, but you—you are not going to eat anything, you are done with eating for the day; that is a ridiculous thing to say, no wonder you have a headache. We have cheese and chocolate but we have no bread. We will have to go out. Around the corner at the silly, fake salumeria, you order for me and eat everything, but you cannot drink. It is done, we go home. Do you want to take a taxi? I ask. We are three blocks from your door. A month ago, from the restaurant, although it was April, we took a taxi three blocks because you had not put on your overcoat and you were freezing. We return; I see that the bottle of wine in its silver canister is half empty. I have become a scold, shaking my finger. Bouncing off the walls, a spaldeen. *One, two, three, aleerie.* When really, it is *one, zero, one, zero.* You ask me about the death of my grandfather. I set up the sugar cubes, the packets, and the saltshaker to show you how I charged down the stairs and threw myself, in my nightgown, at twelve, at my father. I am a little packet of sugar.

Here is another body hurtling through space. It was summer. I was pregnant with Pom. We lived then on a block that led to the park, and I was halfway down the street when I saw a group huddled by the nursery school, mothers—it was mainly mothers—a few nannies, and one or two fathers, unshaven and in shorts. The women wore sundresses, and a breeze lifted their skirts so that the circle of figures looked like a many-colored parachute. As I approached, two women spun toward me, holding up their hands. *Don't look!* One, a woman with grizzled hair I had seen often in the street, took me by the shoulders: *Don't look*, she said. *Turn around.*

A girl had jumped from a sixth-floor window in the building next to the nursery school. The building faced north. The window was a twin of the big window in the living room of our apartment, although our windows faced east. Her body lay on the sidewalk. The women blocked my view, but I had seen her, a scarecrow in brown jeans and a white T-shirt, a blond braid. I thought, she braided her hair. I had braided Louie's hair that morning. And I thought, did she know when the children were dismissed from school? Did she jump then because it was the last moment when they wouldn't see her fall? Three police cars and an ambulance pulled up at the curb. My hands were over my belly, as if I could cover the eyes of the baby. Her heel drummed on my pelvic bone. Do not go to circuses, nor disasters! How strange, I thought, that these women—come to pick up their children at the end of the twentieth century, their shopping in bags slung over their strollers, a bunch of carrots, pasta, milk—would without thinking run to protect me and that I, a tremor passing over my skin, would find when Pom was born an anxiety that has never really left. A frisson. Ah, so sensitive, I hear you say. But you are the same, full of portents, rushing in every direction to make sure that the dark doesn't find you. *On Monsters and Marvels*, by the sixteenth-century surgeon Ambroise Paré, included chapters on the causes of monsters, including "An Example of Monsters That Are Created Through the Imagination," and "An Example of Monsters That Are Formed, the Mother Having Remained Seated Too Long." *Chaque mouvement nous révèle*, wrote Montaigne.

## ESTATE

The things that happen to you, *carissima*, you say. Your story is worse. A hierarchy of stories. The night before, you dreamt that you were lecturing. You are always lecturing, I said. Stop, or I won't tell you. Tell me. I was in a room covered with maps. They were the kind of maps we had in school. Did you have them, too? The maps were colored brown and green and blue. There were ridges where the mountains were indicated. Yes, we had them. In the dream, were the maps all around, were you inside the maps? No, they were behind me, on a wall. There was a lectern. I had a pointer. I was pointing to places on the maps. I spoke for a long time. You always speak for a long time. Do you want me to tell you or not? I was leaning on the long, low dresser, with its wooden tray of treasures, and the silver soap dish, shaped like a bathtub, in which I put my bracelets and earrings so I do not lose them in the bed—remind me to tell you about the glass bracelets I wore years ago, that Colin brought back from India—and I said, what's the point? The silver soap dish belongs to the missing sink. In the winter when it was cold, I took a bath, and you slipped in over me, like a manatee. It was the first time I had used that voice with you, a voice I know well, and is well-known to others. It is an experiment for me, using that voice, the voice of a woman who asks for nothing and by not asking is free.

Come sit, you said. In the half-light on the sofa, I said, the light is always the same, here. And you said, that is because you are always here at the same time, and I said, no—when I came months ago at this time, it was dark, and I have been here in the mornings, but the light is always the same: it is gray light, like Paris. Paris is not always gray, you said. You were telling me your dream about the maps covered with rivers and mountains. Once when you were traveling—you hate traveling, you hate to fly, we talk idly about going somewhere together, and then I say, but you hate to travel, and you say, yes, I hate to travel, and I hate when someone talks to me in an airplane, and I said, I wouldn't talk to you, and you said, not you. But once when you were traveling—it must have been to Italy, you said, the pause between the t and the a pronounced, elongated, the place name in English you hold in your mouth like a sweet or medicine before you swallow—you sat next to a Japanese man. He was very young. A boy, really. He was a mapmaker, for electronics companies: he mapped computer models, who knows what it was. But he also made beautiful drawings of birds flying. A few strokes. He was represented by some galleries, in Tokyo and Cologne, but he had no idea really how to pursue that life; his family had no interest in his drawings. You kept up with him for a few years. And then when your computer crashed and you lost your contacts, you lost him, because you could not exactly remember his name. The thought of the loss distresses you. To lose a person. That small connection, snapped. Because it is now night, you turn on the standing lamp. It is too bright; I turn it a little, away. You have been showing me pamphlets printed in Venice by your great-grandfather. A tiny pair of wings, an angel, a moon and stars: each colophon is indelible and fleeting, the ink like the ink of an octopus, like the birds painted by your Japanese man, who drew maps, who vanished. Who did not even leave a language, because you cannot remember, exactly, his name.

But what does it mean to disappear? The canoe capsized. The river, with its patina of frog spawn, twists toward a vanishing point, a cul-de-sac of last resort. And there, washed up, are the last things, the collapsed table in the garden, the last thing Pascal put together before he disappeared. The last thing I wanted. You did not meet him. He was the nephew of friends. Later, it was the kind of story that surfaced late at night, like a tin can found in the river, the sodden label peeling off: WE MAKE THE BEST OF A GOOD THING. When he arrived from Paris, he would buy a bag of socks and hand them out on the street. What did he do? He wrote position papers about fossil fuel, or he owned a fleet of trucks crossing the Apennines, the Dordogne. What was in those trucks? Who knows. He came to the city four, five times a year. We went to the theater, or he took Pom for a treat. In between he wrote long letters, about Molière, the Seine, the pigeon at his window, its necklace of violet feathers. In the one photograph I have, he is standing on the beach at Mattapoisett, and in the foreground two girls, his cousins, are dancing, his face obscured by their arms. *Il n'y a pas de secret du cœur que nos actions ne révèlent.* A week before he left, he wrote he was arriving on Thursday and was I free? Yes, I said. When? Friday, Saturday, and Sunday. He did not want to go to dinner or to the theater. I was not to tell Pom. Could I do that? Yes. It was the Easter holidays; her father had taken her on a trip. I had hoped of course to see you but it was a week Valeria was here, with some ailment, or her sister, or a parrot on a leash. Did I say how young he was? Thirty-two, maybe thirty-four. The nephew of friends, grown up from the litter of children on the beach.

What are you reading? he asked me, that summer. It was, you will laugh at me, the first time I felt my age. Perhaps that is what he taught me. It was April and chilly. I wore a coat and a shawl printed with birds; he wore a striped school scarf. He had been to school in England, and the boys made fun of him; he was small for his age. We walked east on Seventy-Sixth Street and then into the park, and sat by the Boat Pond, where years later you and I watched the reflection on the water turn from green to red; you teased me because I said *cavallo* when I meant *capello*, and wrote it out for me, a sketch of a horse wearing a porkpie hat—I found it the other day, in a stash of old receipts. We read aloud, bits from the paper, the books we were reading: "A personal relation was a relation only so long as people either perfectly understood or, better still, didn't care if they didn't."

    I cannot accurately describe that trio of days, to you or to anyone else—afterward it was incumbent on me to describe it, for what had happened, actually? When I try to piece it together, it falls apart like a collage pasted with spit. The afternoon in the park, the blurred buds of the magnolias like the bulbs of candelabras. What did we do? His cheeks turned red from the cold, like a child who has been skating in wide circles on a frozen lake. He had forgotten his gloves; he walked with his hands in his pockets. He bought us coffee from a street vendor, and we drank it on the steps of the museum, the steam rising. That day, the Friday before Easter, we saw an exhibit of sixteenth-century tapestries. We stood for a long time looking at God accusing Adam and Eve just as they are wrenched from everything known and beloved, Eve cowering beside Adam, whose foot extended just beyond the beleaved hem of the tapestry. A red cloak and a blue snake. We went back to the house. I made an omelet. We drank Lambrusco, although it wasn't summer yet. We read letters to the editor out loud. "The word *hedgehog* is derived thus: first element from its frequenting hedges; the second element a reference to its pig-like snout." Pascal went upstairs to take a nap, and when I went to wake him, I saw he had carefully folded his sweater and placed his shoes neatly, side by side, before pulling up the duvet. On the bookcase was George's old movie projector, with a hand-lettered sign: DO NOT USE, MAY CATCH ON FIRE!

When he disappeared into thin air a day later, for a long time afterward I thought about the tapestry—Adam's foot, parting the leaves. Try to remember, said his cousin Brigitte. Was there something you missed? He returned on Sunday, on his way to the airport, to have a coffee. He brought a huge lavender plant in a pot. When he arrived, I was trying to set up the new table in the garden, and he did it for me, turning it upside down, unpacking the small screws from the packet. *Voilà, une table.* The geraniums budding, the hellebores done. Goodbye, goodbye, I said. From the airport he sent a message:

Dear Caroline,
I am writing to you first, after our time together, to let you know that I am planning to disappear for awhile. I do not know how long it will be, perhaps six months, or a year. I will be in touch as soon as I can. I will write another email that you will receive, addressed to my family and friends, after this one. I hope you will see me again, when I return, and that that will be possible for you, even as I now have no explanation.

with love,<br>Pascal

Within half an hour the next message arrived. The telephone began to ring. For the first year I wrote every month, then every six months. What happened? asked Pom, a child too used to sudden reversals. In *The Lady Vanishes*, on the train to London, Gilbert says to Iris Henderson, "Can I help?" and she answers, "Only by going away." Pascal's disappearance did not help. I thought, I will go to the Dordogne. I pictured myself in a plain gray coat, carrying a brown paper bag of sandwiches. I will go to Paris. By then the magnolia petals were brown on the lawn, the gaudy tulips had lost track of themselves. In the Conservatory Garden the lilacs had begun. And in time I began to feel I was to blame. Who else? Worse was to think that it didn't matter, that I could have been anyone at all. I was the last person he saw before he left his old life, his life, a life made of bits and pieces. Like a precipice, I was the place from which he felt he could step off into air.

In the kitchen this morning, typing, at the table across from the Japanese drawing of a carp, head down, swimming between the window and the door that leads to the garden. How long has it been there? Who will fix the window caulking, who will repoint the back of the house? Soon, the carp will be swimming in rainwater. I search: mason, plumber, carp, Japanese paintings of carp. There is nothing like the Internet! A pudding filled with plums and prizes on which to break your teeth, little charms, where one thing does lead to another: a tiny camera, a cat by the tail, maybe I can forget the chance that I didn't have. Enough. Buck up, bronco. The children drift downstairs carrying their sleepy dreams. Louie, in a too-tight dress; it is 7:30 in the morning and she wants me to read to her from her prompt script, which I find tucked inside of a copy of *The Periodic Table* I was reading on the subway, at the page when he is taken to prison in the deep snow but has the presence of mind to tuck his notebook with his list of contacts into a snowbank. Oh, for school to be done for the summer. Then at dinner the children were talking about exams. I said, I was the best blue book writer in the east; you haven't read *The Varieties of Religious Experience*? No? So, this sentence brings to mind a similar trope in *The Sound and the Fury*. Click-clack. All those titles with two nouns: *The Mill on the Floss, Sense and Sensibility, The Red and the Black*. In *The Present and the Past*, Megan says, about the hen who is pecking itself to death, "Perhaps it should not do a thing that leads to dying." "I'll skip that scene, if you don't mind," says Etta Place. But there is no help for that, as you would say. And, also: it is not true to say, no telling where it leads. George was quite funny, talking about working with others. "I don't have time for process." The situation—typing while Frank reads upstairs, as he likes to, on his stomach, like a lizard or a crocodile, while my heart is elsewhere; he is too big to be a lizard, drinking the black coffee that I made at six a.m., in the kitchen here with wind bustling in the garden and Pom half-dressed, because she cannot find her school skirt—this morning seems to me not morose but funny. He is here for a week. It is his misfortune, to love me too much, a woman who cannot love anyone unless she is backing herself into an abyss. Read to me, I said, as I drove off in the other direction, safety residing only in being unsafe. In the car between Mattapoisett and Providence, Frank read *The Tempest* aloud to me on the telephone as I drove, his vowels catching in my throat, the phone close to my ear. Once you said, but this is safe, here with me, and I burst into tears. A laugh on the way to the gallows, where I have tucked a list of addresses of old friends in the snowbank.

An email now in my letterbox: Your birthday party went well, for your ninety-year-old friend. As a small child, she was taken to Auschwitz. Now she lives in an apartment over the East River. Her son is a Hollywood producer, and she is estranged from her daughter. I could not come to this party because Esther was there. I could not come to the party because Frank is here. There was the possibility that I could have come to the party with Frank, but that did not arise. You: It would have been impossible to include you, but I kept thinking of you and the conversations we might have had. I think, here is one: The other day, it was Friday, and I was to meet Pom in front of the library before going to the ballet. Louie called. She'd had a nightmare; these nightmares run in the family, Yes, I can hear you saying. These days her conversations are almost solely about her dreams and nightmares. It was a dream about Auschwitz, she said. What else runs in the family? An umbilical cord like a length of barbed wire. We were in the woods, she said, it was very cold. Who was in the woods? I asked. We were, she said. Who is we? Us, she said, Pom and George and me. And you were there. No one else? No, she said, Daddy was not there. He is not usually in my dreams. It was very cold and there was deep snow, and I knew that we were running away, but you said we would be safe. How is this a dream about Auschwitz? I asked. Because it was, that was what the dream was about. I knew it in the dream, and I knew it when I woke up. That's a lot to know, I said. I always remember my dreams, she said. In the dream we were in peril—it was a weird dream, wasn't it? Now I must go upstairs and forget about you. In his blue notebook Michael wrote: *Obscure objects darted among the branches, and first one tree and then the next would bend from the weight of myriad flying creatures lit for an instant among its branches. The air was full with the whir of wings.* The cave was full of bats.

---

A feeling of having lost the thread. A feeling of exhaustion. Of counting my losses and losing my way. Yesterday, on the way back to the city on the parkway, I cried in the car for an hour, great gusts of tears. It was raining hard. I do not know what the tears were for. Grief? Oh please, I thought to myself. But that is not the story I am telling here, is it? Last week at the opera, the set was a raft that twisted on its stanchions. A door opens, the raft is a castle, a boardwalk, a highway, a forest; the planks are the memories of trees. Stories told to avoid telling other stories? Your father slumped in the car—what kind of car was it? What color? That is one story. A conversation with Pom about why she likes broccoli but I don't. But I do like broccoli. The beginning of the story you know: six months after Pom was born, I had my appendix out, after weeks of illness without a diagnosis. After the operation I went to Tulsa, to see an old friend from college. I brought Pom with me. It was the eldest child's birthday. As a small child she was a prodigy. She read at three, wrote sonnets at eight, hummed Bach. This child, who was called Izzy, was the first or second child I knew well. When my first husband and I were married, we often saw this friend, Naomi, and her husband, Daniel. They came with the baby and slept on a mattress on the floor of our apartment on Riverside Drive. I am trying to picture Daniel. He was always carrying something: groceries, a child, a box of tools. He looked uncomfortable in an armchair. We stayed—why, I don't remember—a few times in the "finished" basement of his father's house, which was in a suburb of identical ranch houses, set back from the street, outside Baltimore.

In those days we were playing at being grown-ups. We made careful grocery lists—milk, diapers, orange juice—and sat with the children at the swing set in the park, making more lists, saying look, look, look: at the trees, at the ball, at the dog. We didn't know that the things we needed were not on the list, and if they were on the list, they were written in invisible ink. Twenty years later these years translate into the back of a gold head going out the door, calling over her shoulder, "Well, wish me luck on my exam." My friendship with Daniel was, in its way, a romance. I had left Alastair on a park bench and thought I would never return to him. In the early days, I did not know whether or not I could have a child. Then children were miraculous, the half-moons of their fingernails, their cornsilk hair. Look what we made! I remember a number of years later—or a day later, or ten weeks later; those days are a swarm of mainly physical sensations—closing the refrigerator door with my shoulder because I had a baby on my hip, getting out of a car with George in my arms, feeling the weight of him and his damp mouth on my skin. Daniel's father had two refrigerators in the basement, filled with food. Roasts wrapped first in white paper and then plastic. Bags of peas. Chicken parts. Ice cream. Daniel said, all their friends, everyone from the camps, has two refrigerators and two freezers. His father owned a sausage business. *Traif*, Daniel would say, all the money is from *traif*. He was curt, almost rude with those he had no patience for, which was almost everyone except strangers, to whom he was unfailingly polite, but he had any amount of time for those he loved. He was very angry with me for leaving my first husband, and I did not tell him why, and for a long time he stopped speaking to me. When I came to Tulsa with Pom, who had a different father, the baby made it possible for us to speak again; he loved small children, and cats, who came to him immediately, rubbing their faces on his knees. He had been born in Brazil, and his endearments and imprecations were always in Portuguese.

Daniel was quick in his movements. His eyes were like yours, but smaller. Deep brown, the pupils ringed as if with kohl. His brother whom he loved had died of brain cancer. This for him was a direct assault: the loss wounded him and did not heal. Naomi married him by enveloping him, sweeping him up. It was as if everything that was not Daniel had been a mirage: the Argentinean boyfriend, Oxford. Her endless, self-lacerating love for Declan, whom she had met on a train. At first, Daniel had no patience with us. He was short with me. He smoked cheroots on the balcony with George's father, throwing them into the strip of garden. Then, just as quickly, he loved us, bringing an armload of flowers or a case of wine. Extravagances that he himself had no use for. You like that sort of thing, he said to me. If I listen very hard, even now I can hear his voice in my ear, on the telephone, telling me where he parked the car, so I could come meet him. The caress of it. I did not drive, then. Sometimes he drove me to faraway outlets where we could buy diapers, charcoal, pounds of canned tomatoes and grape leaves, which he loved. Cartons of cigarettes. Our attachment was partly sexual, a heat, but that was inconsequential, he would shrug, par for the course. We never spoke of it. He would touch my back in passing, or my forearm. He wore a leather jacket and smelled of leather and sawdust and cigarettes, which he smoked outside the house. People used to say that, "going out for a smoke." When George was born, the first time they came to see him, he would not put him down—Jorge, Jorge, *meu querido Jorge*, he crooned. No child cried in Daniel's arms. We were novices, with our shopping lists and fold-up cots and stuffed toys, always leaving something behind. I do not know if you took care of Stefano that way, the piles of stuff, the car smelling of old juice, milk in your hair. I imagine not.

You would have not been interested in me then, a baby under my coat, walking in Riverside Park past Eighty-Sixth Street, a leopard-skin coat that was thrown out, later, by mistake. You say, yes, I would have fallen in love with you, and *il cappotto di leopardo*, but I think, no. I was a leopard mother in a leopard skin, carrying a baby to whom I sang for hours by the Hudson. *As I walked out one morning, walking on Bristol Street.* We took the children to the museum and held them up to see the Lorenzettis. They named the fish in the Chinese Pond. They were so small, Izzy and George and Louie, in San Gimignano, where we sat in the piazza, and perhaps you were smoking nearby and Stefano was playing with the pigeons, a day when the American little girls ate ices on the steps of Santa Maria Assunta? Who can know now? It doesn't matter. It was the trip where one side of the road was lit by fireflies and the other side was in darkness.

Last night I cooked the first thing I have cooked for you, an apple cut and sautéed in butter. Pom was spending the night at a friend's. Cooked for you, that is, not for a number of other people with whom you happened to be seated at the table. When your friend Jamie asked you last week how we met—it was a rare evening, out together with a friend—you said we had known each other a long time, a little bit, but for you there was a moment, in Stockholm. A footfall of light coming into the room where you were reading. And you wrote to me, I said. Yes, you said, I wrote to you. As I turned down the flame under the apples, you said, today I had a ridiculous morning. Yes? A man called me on the phone and wanted to meet me for coffee at 7:30 a.m. Who was it? I asked. It was a man I hardly know who accused me of having an affair with his wife. Are you having an affair with his wife? No. I went to bed with his wife once two years ago. That was it. Some emails. Nothing. Nothing? No. Why did he need to meet you at 7:30 in the morning? It was 8:30. You said 7:30. It was 8:30. It was ridiculous for him to approach me. Should I go to bed with his wife, should I not, that is not my problem, it is hers. It is not even his! I think what happened is that they are having troubles, and he accused her of having an affair, and for whatever ridiculous reason she told him about me, probably the truth, and he made it into this thing in his head, when it is nothing, and paid no attention to the actual truth, which is about him, or them, but not about me.

Tuesday. No, Wednesday. In my mind I can see Daniel's feet, the small black hairs on his toes. I began to think, this morning at six when I climb the stairs from the kitchen, intending to make the bed, that it would be nice to imagine I am the still center of the house, but I am more like a ball in a pinball machine, a mouse in a maze, one of those alloys Primo Levi writes about, that you cut or distill and then find out it is not uranium after all, but cadmium, named for the great god Cadmus, who sowed dragon's teeth. It was Cadmus who introduced the Phoenician alphabet to the Greeks, says Herodotus, citing the tripods at the Temple of Apollo. What kind of person finds herself at eight a.m. on a Wednesday morning in New York, on her unmade bed, in ordinary time, her hands over her eyes weeping for the loss of the Linear A language, the written word of the Minoans? Thomasina, weeping for the loss of the libraries—"All the lost plays of the Athenians . . . how can we sleep for grief!" I click on file after file, an arrow moving backward. It is because you have not loved your mind enough that it is restless, says Krishna. It was Talos, a nephew of Daedalus, who was the first person to make a maze, for his pet rat. He was eight years old. When Daedalus tried to punish him for being too clever by throwing him from the Acropolis wall, Athena turned Talos into a partridge, a bird who flies close to the ground. Each link is another hieroglyph, a pen drawing of one thing or another lost or left—shoes, laces, a notebook, my hat at the restaurant, the eye of the needle through which history paces. Nothing is sacred, says the oracle. We cannot be sure, says the etymologist, of the evolution of "cock and bull." A cock-and-bull story? *Coq-à-l'âne*, cited in Randle Cotgrave's *A Dictionarie of the French and English Tongues*, 1611: "An incoherent story, passing from one subject to another." Cosgrave contradicts him: the expression "cock-and-bull" derives from the proximity of two coaching inns, The Cock and The Bull, at Stony Stratford in Buckinghamshire, the place-name indicating its location at a stony ford on the old Roman road, now the A5.

What did Louie say, looking up from her book? When Hera turned Io into a cow, Zeus took pity and surrounded her with violets, so she would have something pretty to eat! And now in Greek violets are called ions—*so* nice, Mama! I am a grown woman with children, weeping in bed on a Wednesday morning. How many dragon's teeth did Cadmus sow? Jack be nimble. The rhyme is just out of reach—how many . . . ?

When we bought this house where I live now with Pom, we exchanged long views for interior views. A bad bet, a woman who leaves her husbands, not to mention lovers, because she does not know the least thing about love, and who comes with an enormous, heavily mortgaged house, children, three cats, a temper, and spends too much money on clothes. A note from Frank:

> Mab, darling—Probably old hat (tam-o'-shanter) to you, but have you looked at the shark callers of New Guinea re Michael R?—New Scotland, Duke of Drama, and Tabark, to be more geographically precise . . . Spiritual hoo-ha, divination as much as hunting . . .

Then another:

I won't do this again if you don't want me to.

              xx

              F.

And then, six hours later:

Do you know that in the last five weeks you haven't bothered to respond to a single email I have sent you?

In the afternoon Pom is doing a crossword puzzle in the car on the way home from her softball game. What is a diamond in the sky? A kite. Do you know what that is, baby? It's one of those things that goes up in the air. A line on the back of an envelope in that apartment on Park Avenue, full of haints and little girls teasing the dead. Where did Pascal disappear to? Later this evening you write to me, *back from far out at sea: navigating in the dark, among big waves and fish.* A kite, swooping over the hedge, a present from Mickey Mickeranno. Hold the string tight, and stand here in front of me and take the strain, the years like white storm birds.

This evening, the lump in my throat, without which I do not know who I am. In the Michael Rockefeller wing at the Met, the Bis poles point upward, the roots of the tree scrape heaven, the boat to the land of the dead is at the top of the tree. Do we grow up, or down? I sent you an email this morning, after an email and a call from you: you are out for the evening, who knows where. Again and again, as if hypnotized, I need to re-create heartbreak, like a madwoman carrying a house of popsicle sticks, walking up and down the hill, one foot in front of the other. When I think of separating from Frank, I think of bark peeled off a living tree. We have known each other for thirty years. Years after this, the table where I work, the house itself, the dashboard of the car, became littered with peeled bark, birch, and sycamore, the periderm stripped from the heartwood, a snake shedding its skin from its jeweled eye to its iridescent scales. If I look I can feel that desire pulsing, moth wings against the shavings, bones whittled down to letters of the alphabet. It is true, perhaps, that I have no scruples. But, perhaps not. Perhaps I have too many. The wrath that bore an apple bright. Look, there are Madame de Vionnet and Lambert Strether, rounding the bank again; the river must twist just there; I must wave my handkerchief to them!—they, too, are searching now, along the riverbank, for some proof. No one just disappears. The governor's plane is circling overhead, a puzzle piece that should be easy to fit because it has a distinctive splotch of blue, but as yet, it fits nowhere. Perhaps it is because I am trying, we are trying, I almost wrote, but of course you are not trying, you have not been putting me in a taxi for twenty-five years. Or you have.

I take Pom to lunch with her friend Violet and her mother, Amy, who is dating a Chinese man. She tells me where he went to school; we are the kind of people who know this, or want to know this, a certain kind of American, although we have not been to school in thirty years. The girls eat profiteroles. The girls know all about him; they have agreed that if they are going to have stepfathers, it should be educational: a Chinese stepfather fits this bill. Today was Last Day at school. It is wonderful how clear it is: they were in seventh grade, now they are in eighth grade. Once you are in eighth grade, no matter how much you might want to, you can't go back. Not ever. The mothers cry at the start, at "Jerusalem," and the girls cry at the end of the ceremony—they are on the cusp of tears, but if they carry it very carefully, they won't spill it, not yet. I am reading *The African Queen*. I am up to the place where Allnut says to Rose, "I fort, Miss, 'ow we might find somewhere quiet be'ind an island where we couldn't be seen. Then we could talk about what we could do." "I should think that would be best," said Rose.

When you moved with your mother and sister to New York, the building where in the long, dim, ghost-ridden apartment my cousin Sarah and I conducted séances—a game for sleepovers, the crystal ball made out of a goldfish bowl, the Ouija board jumping from number to letter—there was a girl who lived across from the museum who was in love with you. Who were we trying to raise from the dead? We knew no one yet who had died but shadowy great-grandparents, whose lives we didn't think to imagine. When you walked to school through the park, she followed you, twenty paces behind, stopping when you stopped. She was a plain girl, with something beautiful about her. How old were you? Sixteen? You invited her to dinner. You'd cooked the meal yourself. Your mother and sister went to the movies. She did not come. A story about desire creating desire, that answering desire wanting to meet what is offered, the mirror that becomes a magnet. The filings jump. What kind of animal would you be, if you could come back as an animal? A zebra. An ocelot. Another game we played, in the building where green leatherette peeled off the elevator walls. I have spent a lot of time peeling things with my fingernail—scabs, wallpaper, the scales of a fish with their sharp beveled edges. When I was a child I bit my fingers until they bled, tiny starbursts of blood seeping through the graying bandages.

*Lo sai: debbo riperderti e non posse.*
*Come un tiro aggiustato mi sommuovo*

You know I should renounce you and I cannot.
With trigger sureness, everything confounds me.

With trigger sureness, everything confounds me. In that way we are similar, you and I, with our loyalties, with our inability to leave ourselves behind, our passionate prevarications, which allow us to be elsewhere.

    Now it is June. School is out finally, an ebbing tide of blue serge. Pom has gone to Maine for a week, and then will be taken to camp, and I have come up here near the ocean to stay with Frank in the little house he rents while my house is rented out. Did I tell you that? I am assuming you knew; we never talk of such things. He is ill. Not too ill but ill. Of course, I am not really helping, I am strewing things around, and he is insisting on hoisting himself up to make me coffee; that is the way it is with us. It is very hot here; it must be hot in the city—you refuse adamantly to go anywhere, and then you go off, not saying where, to visit a countess or some old acquaintance who is dying. In the glider I watch my hands start to clench and unfold like the water lily—which Frank calls a lotus—that I pulled from Vagabond Pond. My right hand does not know my left. In this landscape, the pond, the woods, the road into town, I see myself coming and going, a child in a blue bathing suit, a teenager, clawing at my hands. What am I holding and letting go of? As if my body were a map, fingers numb, *the sheer inability* to get from one place to another without getting stuck, the needle slipping and catching. The boat continually capsizing. As usual I get everything wrong. On the porch is a mug filled with short-stemmed shrub roses. A woman typing on a screened porch behind a hedge on a Sunday morning, who has no idea what is good for her. The koan is: I do not know what I want to know. No. The koan is: I do not know what I do not want to know. The nurse, who wore an old-fashioned white cap, tut-tutted when she saw my bruised hand. The other hand? she asked. Jesus Christ, said Daniel. The pockmarks where they had tried to insert the needles looked like bird tracks that had bled under the skin. Black starbursts. Yes, he said. Use the other hand, Daniel said. He was holding the baby.

He was holding the baby. Morphine dripped into my hand and up my arm. In New Guinea the Asmat people live in houses that are built on stilts, often as high as twenty-five meters off the ground. Reading this, I think, how is it possible? They live in tree houses. After the beautiful Bis poles are erected, they stand in a grove of nutmeg trees, so it is as if certain of the trees have sprouted wings, their roots wings and the branches shorn away, as the heads of novitiates are shorn. Ssh. The morphine dripped into the capillaries of my arm. Daniel held the baby.

*I had a little nut tree, nothing would it bear, but a silver nut meg and a golden pear. The owl and the pussycat went to sea.* That's where we were in the middle of the night in the hospital in Tulsa with the kind, wide-faced nurses: an animal family, the baby perplexed, wide awake, her blue eyes cornflowers, Daniel crooning under his beard. The Asmat were headhunters. The Bis poles avenged the death of a soul taken by headhunting; they believe that all deaths are the result of sorcery. To prevent the dead from coming back and haunting the village, the little girls have their fingers cut off, one by one. How can that be? It is. You knew that—when can I tell you something you don't already know?

But we feel that, too—it is impossible, how can it not be, for the spirit to leave the body. All that work of breathing, the habit of it, gone? The body of the canoe carries a turtle, and an okom, a dangerous water spirit. The white-capped nurses came and went, my mind beat against itself; the nothing that is not there and the nothing that is, but there is no snow here, it is summer. My mind was a thumbprint on the white wall. Ssh, said Daniel to the baby, as we hovered between the living and the dead. I didn't want to be there, it was not what I meant, at all.

I had come for a birthday and ended up in the emergency room of a small city hospital. In the ICU the nurses came and went. Time for a hundred indecisions. Daniel held the baby. In the hall outside the lit-up ICU, floating like a spaceship through the night, there was a stack of old magazines. To amuse her, Daniel tore a page from a magazine and rolled it into a ball. It was the way my father had taught me to build a fire, tearing and balling up *The New York Times*, the print smearing my hands black in the gigantic fireplace, big enough to roast a baby in. The baby could not crawl or walk, not yet. Daniel took his jacket and put it on the floor, and put the baby on the jacket and rolled the ball to her, and she batted it with her hands. Can you roll it back, sweetheart? he crooned. The baby batted the ball with her head and put the ball in her mouth. No, said Daniel. Do you want to make a ball, sweetheart? He was a bear father talking to the human child. On the canoe of the gurney I was the shore and an island, far out at sea.

But why this—front and center—a story about Daniel? Why this compulsion to tell you? When we first met, you coaxed from me another story. I didn't ask! I can hear you saying. Or I had a compulsion, to tell you. A journey over land, not water, into a forest shiny with snow. *Dimmi*, you said. You never ask. When I told you that story, my father was alive. But as you would be the first to point out, there are stories, and there are stories. The corner of the page folded, a little sail, marking a place where the book was put down. At the corner, when the young girl asks the woman on the curb, "Does the number five bus stop here?" a woman wearing a green turban and an overcoat, carrying three shopping bags, she says, "Well, I think it does, but you know, angel, I don't know everything." I come back to the city, because Louie is home now, and the next morning we go to Tender Buttons, the store on Sixty-Second Street that sells only buttons. Once, around the corner, you bought me a pair of green gloves. I had not been there in years, but there was a period when I went often. What could I have been looking for, among so many fastenings? I remember Louie choosing some enamel buttons for a pink cardigan her grandmother had knitted for her, from among the antique buttons with pictures of bears stamped on their round faces. The same child who calls in the middle of the night because her boyfriend whom she has tried to break up with has told her he will kill himself if she leaves him. He will not kill himself, I tell her. Cross my heart, I think, and hope to die. I am looking for buttons for a white coat that I will wear because I think you will like it. Why, asked Pom, the child who long ago batted back the ball made from a torn page of *People* magazine, the starlets wrinkled and creased, does Louie have to feel sad and worried for so long beforehand? There will be time to be sad afterward. True. There is always time to be sad afterward.

Last night I fell asleep with my clothes on, the radio on, the lights on. The house humming, of all things, "Tea for the Tillerman," and then, a radio two-for-one, "Wild World": hope you have a lot of nice things to wear. I woke at four thirty in my dress and shoes. Where had I been? That night on the gurney I drifted down the river. The baby batted back the paper ball in the ICU, and began to cry. The sound of her crying pricked the morphine haze, and I tried to get off the gurney, and a nurse, who had been there all along, held me down. Daniel picked up the baby and held her on his lap, and the baby began to tear the magazine from which he had torn a page—*Splitsville for Madonna!*—into gaudy strips, which fell around them like leaves. It was a tall stack of magazines. There was no one else in the ICU. In the twelve hours we were there, in which time my stomach was pumped twice and I was given an enema, so that by the end I felt like a snake composed only of openings, a conduit or pipe, a pipe organ, played by the trio of nurses who took turns holding me down; the baby, sitting on Daniel's lap, had ripped every one of the magazines to shreds. I tried to get up, a spirit leaving the body. The nurses held me down.

In 1903, Topsy the elephant, who belonged to the Forepaugh Circus at Coney Island, attacked a keeper who fed her a lit cigarette. The circus management decided to put her down. She was twenty-eight. They began by tying her to the bars of her cage. She had killed three men, including a second abusive keeper, in three years. The first method that occurred to them was hanging. From what? How? It was the age of invention. That year inventions included the collapsible periscope, the hearing aid, and the teddy bear, invented in Brooklyn by Morris Michtom, a toy store owner who found himself moved by a true story in which Teddy Roosevelt, on a hunting trip in Mississippi, declined to shoot and kill a tied black bear. He said it was unsportsmanlike. Instead of hanging, Topsy was electrocuted. The electrocution was carried out by the Edison Illuminating Company of Brooklyn. Thomas Edison's factory in Menlo Park in 1887 had "a stock of almost every conceivable material," including

> eight thousand kinds of chemicals, every kind of screw made, every size of needle, every kind of cord or wire, hair of humans, horses, hogs, cows, rabbits, goats, minx, camels . . . silk in every texture, cocoons, various kinds of hoofs, shark's teeth, deer horns, tortoise shell . . . cork, resin, varnish and oil, ostrich feathers, peacock's tail, amber, rubber, jet . . .

By January 1904 the archive also included a film strip of the electrocution of an elephant. Before the current was switched on, Topsy was fed carrots laced with potassium cyanide. In the film she twists for several seconds after she falls on fire to the ground. Fifteen hundred people watched. She fell "without a trumpet or a groan."

In the film *Voyage to Italy*, Ingrid Bergman goes by herself on a tour of the volcanic plains near Naples. The guide says, "See?" He lights a cigarette, and smoke billows and blurs the outlines of what ignites. I had not seen the movie before, I have not seen the movie we are in before—sometimes, as last night, a bad movie—but nonetheless, here we are. She says to her husband, "I realized for the first time that we, we're like strangers," and he answers, "Yes, it's a strange discovery to make. Now that we're strangers, we can start all over again at the beginning. Might be rather amusing, don't you think?" Years later I will say to someone who is not you, whom I also will not marry, perhaps we could be covered with ash, like lovers at Pompeii, a man whose mother liked the story of Pliny, author of thirty-seven books on the natural world, who sailed across the gulf to the smoky beach and was asphyxiated by the conflagration. Yesterday in Oklahoma a tornado ripped apart an elementary school, a playground, and five square blocks of a residential neighborhood. "We've never seen anything like this," said Pete Owens, who until a few hours ago owned a 7-Eleven that was leveled by the twister. "If I was still inside there, I'd be a goner."

In the ICU, now and again, Daniel walked the baby down the corridor in order to play with the soda and candy machine. He looked taciturn and wild, someone whom it would be a mistake to second-guess. Your wife, they said, to him, referring to me, and he left it—it was easier, he told me, not to get into it. And besides, he also said, what difference could it make?—a remark I trod carefully around as, when the children were small, we were always on the lookout, trying to keep them from sharp objects and sorrow. All the years he did not speak to me were hard for him, but because he was stubborn above all else, it was impossible for him to retreat. In the ICU with the baby, love which had been put aside entered the room and filled it, like a helium balloon, and we held on to it and kept afloat, while the baby let go of ballast and littered the floor with paper. Over those years in which we did not speak, I wrote to him but tore up the letters, as I knew he would not read anything I sent him. None of that mattered now. Except that his anger and stubbornness, his rage, his recalcitrance, were a warning, despite his patience with the baby, who thirteen years later, eating supper in the kitchen where orchids filled the window and the fiddleheads were starting in the rocky garden in early May, would say to me, what happened to him?

Stories, says Victor, the guru, the man in the moon, with his little notebook, are the way we keep things straight. In one version of this story I am walking toward you, and as I type this, you recede, a man in a Chesterfield coat, growing smaller and smaller, a *mise en abyme* beloved by Gide, who said, "Everything that needs to be said has already been said. But since no one was listening, everything must be said again," Gide, who loved not men but what devoured them, the ouroboros whose beginning is its end. In the subway on Friday I sat next to a man reading a book about Magritte. He was looking at the pictures. We looked at them together. The lit-up house. The clouds. The floating blue eye, to which nothing has to be explained, that sees everything and nothing. An example of wishful thinking: a child's plea to simply be found out and get it over with, the relief of a child who wants to be caught lying, who wants to be stripped of his cloak of invisibility, who says, look at me! As when two weeks ago Frank sat looking at me and I wanted him to say, tell me about Lorenzo. He said, instead, angrily, a bit later, "There is no sign of me in your room; it's as though I do not exist. You had a photo, and it is gone."

---

*She stands in the vestibule inside a stand of boxwood. Has she made the boxwood maze herself? She has hidden things: a muddy book, a shoehorn. There is one door; no, two. The smell is thick and metallic, a porch screen smell, her nose against it. Her eyes are screwed tight. She is the size of a cat; no, a mouse. Catskin's white dress fit in a nutshell. Someone has asked her to wait. A is for Apple. She is too young to take another step without permission; she cannot step down the two concrete steps, nor enter the house. But it does not feel like stuck, it feels like waiting. She has been left there, by whom, for what reason, and the space around her is pearly gray; the concrete steps are a darker gray and smell of damp, because someone had been* watering the boxwood. The leaves were glistening and the roots were wet, she could not see the roots, but she knew they were there, the damp roots with their brown tendrils, almost like hair, in the mulch. Her hair was tied back with a pink ribbon. On the stairs the water had made shapes, like teeth or the distant mountains in a Japanese scroll painting. She is a small child waiting under the trellis by the boxwood as she has been told to do. Someone said, wait here. Or, wait there. She is wearing a white cotton dress with pink smocking. A few threads of the smocking have come undone. Don't pull the thread, said Ariadne. Pulling it will lead nowhere. Is she wearing a white dress? Her straight almost black hair falls below her shoulders. Her hair has been brushed very hard, she is still feeling the pull on her scalp. Later, when she is older and learns about electric shock therapy, she will feel the sting of her hair being pulled by the brush, each hair a burning filament. Topsy the elephant in the circus tent. She had ridden on an elephant, in a red sweater. Hold on tight, said the elephant man. She had forgotten, and then there it was, a photograph. A little grainy, her hair held back by a slide. Pixelated. She could remember the smell of the saddle, and the thick pungent smell of the elephant. She is gigantic in the boxwood, which smells smoky and green. A leaf makes a green cap on her fingertip. Inside herself, the child is terrible and huge. She cannot get out. The child is five or six, or even younger; she is standing between the steps stained with damp and an oak door, which is closed. The door has a pane of glass. There is a keyhole in the lock plate for an old-fashioned key, and above that, a new brass plate with a new lock. It is late May or June. It is June. A dense climbing hydrangea hugs the trellis. It is July. The little girl in the doorway, smelling the boxwood as if she is spelling water in her hand. If she spells water, she will find her way out of the boxwood. The door is shut. She cannot open it. Instead, she spells wait-here, a child who grows up to sit in the audience at a performance of Twelfth Night, listening to songs: What is love? 'Tis not hereafter, / Present mirth, hath present laughter. That is the wrong play. Rather, Give me that man / That is not passion's slave and I will wear him / In my heart's core. The play is "The Mousetrap." It doesn't make no nevermind, she knows what she doesn't know. She is standing on the steps waiting to be told what to do next by someone who has disappeared. Someone will fetch her, or not. Someone will fetch her when he brings the car around. That is what people said, He'll bring the car around. This was a long time ago, the child is alone on the steps. Children were left to their own devices. She might have been there for five minutes or ten, or one, or half an hour. A day. Other things were attended to. Ordering groceries, writing a letter, answering the telephone. Poor hobbyhorse whose epitaph is "For oh, for oh, the hobby-horse is forgot." The telephone was attached to the wall; if you were on the phone, you were on the phone. She is wearing a white dress with off-white smocking, and brown shoes. The shoes are scuffed and too heavy. They were made in France. Later her own children wore those shoes, even though the buckle was still hard to manipulate. They could not put on the shoes themselves, as she could not. She knew how to tie her shoelaces, her father had shown her to make two rabbit ears. Poor rabbit, his ears tied up. But it was hard to put the latch of the buckle inside the tiny hole. Do it yourself, he said. She tried. A Girl Scout. What did the Brownies say?

> Their mystic art, as may be found
> On pages now in volumes bound,
> Was quite enough to bear them in
> Through walls of wood and roofs of tin

    The girl in the doorway with the little green caps on her fingers, who bit her nails for twenty-five years, who was a Brownie for about five minutes, because she did not want to look in a mirror made of tinfoil, can feel the caps on her fingers now, as the sprinklers wave their long fingers over the lawn. At home, where she has never been, she has two felt finger puppets, a dragon and a lion. At the Scuola di San Giorgio degli Schiavoni, where Saint George harasses the dragon in Carpaccio's picture of the Vision of Saint Augustine, the little dog before the cabinet of curios—a shell, a pair of scissors, an astrolabe—wags his tail, like the Victor dog on the record label: Adamant needles bear down on him from / Whirling of outerspace, too black, too near— / But he was taught as a puppy not to flinch. The little girl was taught not to flinch. Not seen, not heard, can you be sure, it doesn't hurt, because it didn't happen. What's to come is still unsure. Standing in the doorway with her finger puppets, she hears the whir of insects in the boxwood. Lift the latch.

> *No hasp can hold, no bolt can stand*
> *Before the Brownie's tiny hand;*
> *The sash will rise, the panel yield,*
> *And leave him master of the field.*

Half a century later, in the same body, remarkable as that is, as impossible, at Columbus Circle outside the Sixtieth Street subway exit, she listens to swallows natter in the boxwood hedges planted on each side of the staircase. Now, if she were to breathe the air under the trellis for too long, the damp would seep into her lungs, she would drown; but she will not stand there much longer, although it seems like a long time, now, and it seemed so then. Who is she waiting for? What did the Brownies say?

> *The eel, the craw-fish, leech, and pout*
> *That watched them from the starting out.*

The boat tipped over. Behold also the ships, which though they be so great, and are driven of fierce winds, yet are they turned about with a very small helm, whithersoever the governor listeth. His master's voice. Time stops when you wait, but it does not; even waiting propels *you forward, and we are elsewhere, a space that fills with letters that spell* wish you were here. *In the file marked Letters from Lunatics:*

> A fortune teller has written a postcard to say that Michael is alive and is living on a small houseboat in the Ganges River. She says that Michael is very happy and would like to be left alone.

> A man who has been in the hospital after a car crash has awoken from a coma, during which Michael came to him in a dream, bearing a knapsack full of fruit. When he emptied the knapsack it was full of jewels. Michael told him he was going to bury them. If the Governor will send one thousand dollars the writer will tell him where the jewels are buried.

*Oh, if only you could pack up your sorrows, and give them all to me. Press the keys. The picture postcards scattered in the Arno, and Lucy Honeychurch says something has happened. How far is it to swim? She waited in the boxwood, and grew up to say she would not be someone who would wait in the doorway. That is what she said. A bull was bitten by a mouse, says Aesop.* Opimum bovem resupinatum in stramento arrodere mus coepit et dentibus multa carne densum femur lacerare. *Paw the ground. She is a girl in a smocked white dress pulling at a thread in a boxwood maze, a girl with a white bull's head. A girl writing on a tablet, white chalk snaking across the black ground. Yes, says Septimus to Thomasina, I think you are the first person to think of this. The world about to fall to pieces. She is not waiting for you.*

---

After a week apart you text me: Call me after the ballet. I wait for Lionel to come out of the State Theater in his pink-and-red kimono and his owl glasses, and put him in a taxi. How can I get away from my mother? he asks. During *Firebird* I resisted the impulse to hold his hand. I say, it was ballet that taught me to shine my shoes. In eighteen months he will be dead. I am annoyed at the flurry of texts. I want to go home but instead call from the street. Where am I? On Sixty-Fifth Street. Cross the street, and walk on the east side of the street. Are you asking me to cross the street? Yes, you are, you are asking me to cross the street. We go to the idiotic salumeria and sit at the counter which is too bright, and you put your hand on my knee. We are strangers. I have nothing to say to you, a man in a black polo shirt late at night in the West Seventies, around the corner from a restaurant that no longer exists above the flower shop that no longer exists, where in our twenties Alastair and I ate three times a week, and the reason why I have never since ordered nor cooked a chicken paillard. And then you kiss me voraciously on the street corner. The next day you arrive at 11:30, and kiss me in the kitchen. I am still wearing my raincoat, and you say, take off your coat. Why are you wearing your coat in the kitchen? And you laugh at my clothes, untying the orange ribbon of my blouse. Who are you, who arrives and sits on the broken bamboo sofa in the kitchen, who takes me upstairs and does not speak, and then an hour later admires the garden almost wordlessly? The wax flowers of the Solomon's seal, the coral bells, the ajuga veined with lavender, the pumpkin vine. Now in the summer we have lightning bugs, I say. You look quizzical. Fireflies. What is firefly in Italian? *Lucciola*. But it is also the name for prostitute. And then you leave, for God knows where. Although I do know where. In bed you asked me, are you cold, or just shy?

Like a Japanese lantern left on the lawn, a joke: A man has written to you, the Palazzo N——, which belonged to your grandparents, or your great-grandparents, is for sale, in Gargnano. I look it up on the map. Do you want to buy it? In the week before we part we discuss the palazzo, how we will live in it, what we will do with it. I say, it will be excellent, it will be so big we can live together and never see each other! You say, I do not want to live in the palazzo and never see you. We are in the park. We entered through the Merchants' Gate and exit on Seventy-Second Street through the Women's Gate. It would be nice to live in a villa, I say. You say, it's not a villa, it's a palazzo, baby. When I embarked on this letter, I thought: nutmeg tree. I thought: in one hundred days this will be done. Nothing will it bear. And now it has turned into something else. An absence. I think what I love is the panic. A love of being abandoned, that evergreen, because there is no believable alternative. And one must love something.

After you left I wrote three letters, each one saying this is impossible: I cannot do this, I am not asking you to change but I cannot continue. I delete them. And then you text me again: Every moment lovely, I could have listened to you talk about your plants for hours. A garden is the best metaphor.

It is Sunday, windy and raining. I put the carpet in the garden to air it out, and forgot it stupidly, so now it will take ages to dry, Hardy's lines a lasso over the chairs, clocks and carpets left on the lawn all day; the sense of being turned inside out, always a little shameful: a day when you wear your shirt inside out is not a good day. Years ago at school we went to watch—what was it, Halley's Comet?—in a field bordered by oak trees, and nearby was a house that had been demolished. Had there been a fire? One half of the house was sheared off, so that you could see, as in a doll's house, a room, or half a room, a table and cabinets, a bed. When we left, there was a thunderstorm. The lightning illuminated the porcelain sink, a standing lamp, a mirror.

A few days ago, before I left for Maine, Valeria somehow miraculously cured, gone; you said, do you remember you said we needed this like a hole in the head? This is better than a hole in the head, yes? You looked eighteen, your face beautiful against the pillow. The ceiling fan propelled the hot air, a whirligig. Your greyhound was called Bell for the bell curve of his back. Your hand is the size of mine, a fact I find continually curious, as I would a deformity. You drew the bell curve in the air above us. Later, we went to the park. A little boy was playing football with his father. Two dogs chased after the ball; enchanted, he soon began running with the dogs and barking.

Did I learn to drive so I could leave my marriage? But what did I leave? Last night the children made a birthday party for me in the garden. Six different kinds of ice cream. I missed you: it was as if a pain ran through me, a needle piercing my skin. Valmont's dagger. Dying, he turns on the marquis, who loves him. Then he is gone; she removes every trace of maquillage from her face. Sometimes I sense in you a kind of querulousness, an inability to allow things *not to go your way*. I am trying to imagine you in your apartment like a shell, the living room blasted by the air conditioner, the phone ringing. Don't be so hard on me—give me five minutes. The cat is licking my hand as I type. You like singers. I cannot sing, not one song. George brought a speaker out into the garden. "For Halloween buy her a trumpet, and for Christmas, get her a gun." It is not a gun, it's a *drum*, said Louie. But gun is better. So tell him, said George, smoking under the hydrangea. The cat has her nose on my foot, at the end of the bed, among the rumpled sheets. Yesterday, I went to see the bronze boxer at the Met, excavated in 1885 from the Baths of Constantine near the Quirinal Hill. Go, you said. But you did not have time to go with me. The sculptor used different alloys to show the boxer's wounds: he was bleeding from his left arm and from his thigh, a plum-sized bruise under his right eye. He looked exhausted, malleable, hurt. It was almost impossible to resist touching him. I wonder what you love so much in him and whether it is what I love? You prize what? Imperviousness. But when you see a hole in my blouse, you say, it is better, more beautiful, where the moths had their supper! It will be ninety-six degrees in New York by noon. Tomorrow I go to Maine, to visit Emma for a few days before I pick up Pom at camp, avoiding any road I have taken before, and so will end up in a rigamarole of towns outside Portland. Stroudwater, Nasons Corner, Riverton. And then follow the coast road toward Rockport.

The *what* of this was a letter to you to keep my heart intact. Maybe I could find out where I wanted to go. A purpose undiminished, or perhaps ironically underscored by my decision to leave, to not speak to you, a decision fraught with implications. Will we see each other two weeks, two months from now, and then not again? Unlikely. Here is a story then, which I longed to tell you, but could not. Yesterday I drove the seven hours to Maine. I had hoped you would call on the drive—but you did not. I did not call you back when you called on my birthday. Now I am berating myself. In Maine there will only be a "landline"; how strange to still call it that, as if the rest of the time we are at sea, holding our walkie-talkies, our ship-to-shore radios; the cosmos calling: how are you? Will you answer, too? A girl, snow in her hair, who has spent decades waiting for one phone call or another. I was two hours early for the ferry, a kind of miracle, as if I had created those two hours, a hole in the hedge of the day. By another miracle there was a parking space, and when I went to buy the ticket the girl at the counter was kind and told me where I could find a bakery: I wanted to bring a pie to North Haven. The street was almost deserted in the heat. There was a used bookstore on Main Street, full of old penny dreadfuls and maps of Maine, cool inside. The bookstore smelled of mold and damp, and like a person in a dream, I began to pick books from the shelves: *Trixie and Topsy*, "the story of a delightful and dreadful little girl who tormented her parents and relations"; a book of Nantucket ghost stories; a Norwegian novel, *The Lion Woman*; a Tauchnitz Classics set bound together with a ribbon, *The Diary of an Idle Woman in Italy*. The packed shelves looked as if not a soul had touched them in forty years. At the register, the proprietor handed me another book—a Tauchnitz, identical to the journal, so at first I thought it was another volume. (He had rearranged the package so "the first volume should be on top.") He was a man of about eighty, wearing a T-shirt that said HARBORMASTER. A Texas man, he said, who comes to Maine in the summer. We agreed that it was hot. It was over one hundred degrees yesterday in New York, I said. Better here, we agreed. Perhaps you'd like this too, miss, I'll just throw it in. A guide to the lakes of Northern Italy, including Lake Garda, a tiny map on the flyleaf. Yes, please, I told him. Later we would discover on that map the address of the palazzo. One volume with a stamp from a bookshop in Venice, in Dorsoduro, where I once spent a pocket of time hiding from the mist and pretending to read the spines of books I cannot read. A little glimmer, Morse code, a fortune cookie. When I walked out of the bookshop, carrying my bags—for I had bought a pie, an enormous loaf of bread, and a pair of green pants at a thrift shop—I was almost completely happy: a splurge standing on the head of a pin, balanced on the hot street, with an hour to wait for the ferry.

The ferry to North Haven takes one hour and fifteen minutes. After I brought my bags from the car, I sat on a bench by the huge green jaws of the ferry dock. A little scene occurred at the curb. A very large fat girl who could have been any age from twenty to forty was trying to coax someone out of a blue Volvo station wagon. Her voice was low and insistent, murmuring, Don't you want to come out of the car, Bob? We're going on the ferry. Inside the car a man was growling. There was a second woman beside the car, thin to the point of emaciation, a woman in her eighties, in a golf skirt, sneakers, a white blouse. A woman you could see anywhere, or almost anywhere, Palm Beach, Nantucket, here, at the North Haven Ferry. Lois is going to park the car and then we will go on the ferry. From inside the car the very old man growled at her again. At first it is hard to see him: the girl is so huge that she blocks the view inside the car entirely, but when she moves aside, we see he is strapped into the passenger seat, wearing a kind of harness. The harness is bright blue. Lois is standing by the car. She has one hand on a shopping cart, which is full of flowers: flats of impatiens and marigolds. The fat girl reaches into the car and takes Bob's arm. She tells him again that he needs to get out of the car because Lois *needs to park the car*. In a sudden flash of inspiration, she says, The car isn't going on the ferry, Bob. Lois is going to *leave* the car in the parking lot and then we will get on the ferry *without* the car. In the car, Bob relents a little. He stops growling. The girl is right: he is afraid they are going to take the car on the ferry and leave him on the dock. He pushes her away with one hand, with unexpected force. She is a big girl, but she staggers. Lois, by the car, stands absolutely still. Next to me on the row of benches are two men in baseball caps and khakis, large, well-fed men in their mid-seventies. Lois is looking at Bob, and not looking at him. She is wearing two gold bangle tennis bracelets and a pale blue bucket hat. The car with Bob in it is six feet away from us, but we know there is nothing we can do to help. We avoid looking at each other. We sit quietly, watching. There is no way not to watch. The girl, who is wearing an enormous pink tank top with spaghetti straps that dig into her shoulders, has a rose tattoo on her left shoulder. As we watch, she reaches into the car and yanks Bob up out of his seat. It is a yank executed with minimum fuss. She has to get him out of the car. The ferry is leaving in ten minutes. The yank unbalances Bob so that he cannot pull himself back but instead, wobbling on his feet, half in and half out, he falls forward. She catches him on her huge breasts. There, there, she says. She guides Bob, a stick figure, who is wearing a red polo shirt and plaid Bermuda shorts, without a belt, the band of his boxers exposed in the North Haven Ferry lot, to his walker. Watching, we forgive the fat girl everything, the forgotten belt, the yank. Without looking at either of them, Lois gets into the Volvo. Until she returns, Bob does not take his eyes from the spot where the car has sat idling. When Lois comes back, she is carrying a Nantucket basket handbag big enough to carry a small dog, and she is still holding the car keys. The fat girl, who has continued to murmur, to console, as Bob stands at the walker, tugging at his shorts, does not look at Lois, who takes command of the shopping cart full of flowers.

Why this little story? It is an unbearable story. Why tell it to you? This morning I woke up at six with the familiar clench in my chest and thought, I must learn how to untie the knot to which I affix your name. On the ferry I went to the upper deck and watched the coastline recede, green as a line of magic marker. The ferry was not crowded. I left my bags, the books, the pie I bought, the bottles of wine for Emma, who lately seems oddly destitute, on my seat. It is July; the sun is a kite high in the sky. Should I have called you back on my birthday? I need to work fast. Somewhere, in another world, snow is falling, and I am in a hotel room, cutting a snowflake out of a sheet of hotel writing paper with nail scissors, humming a song I pivoted around for twenty-five years until you stepped onto the ice. Not again. A is for Alastair, a vanishing point, a laser beam. How many angels on the head of a pin? Are these stories addressed to you or are they "real stories," that is, stories that are not written to *just one person*, even if that person is you, who—if you will read them—may find them beyond boring? *Po' troppo, tutto questo, no?* The things you wanted, I bought them for you. Perhaps you would like to order a chicken sandwich and a glass of milk? How impossible it is to remember everything. Poor Topsy. I dreamt I looked into the water from the ferry dock and saw your face pleating on the current.

Yesterday Emma took me on a walk around Burnt Island at low tide. As we rounded the cove, a maple strangled by poison ivy, the vine thick as my wrist. Poison ivy, she told me, grows only in places that have been disturbed. You and I have retreated into silence, for which we have no language, as Bob in the car has no language, a man who was—I am making this up but it's something like this I'm sure—a banker, who until very recently *went to the office*, is wearing a blue harness and holding on to a walker, who has to be reassured that he will not be left behind. That is something people used to say, too: is he still going to the office? No one goes to the office. I am typing under the trees at Mullen Cove, at North Haven, Maine. The route reminded me of driving to see Alastair, when I was so distraught it was hard to drive, and because of that, as I said, I chose the longest possible route in order to calm down before I crossed into southern Maine. At one town there had been a fair the day before. The gaily colored flags were still up on the mansard of the tiny music school. I thought, just stop, live here. In the worst kind of moments I abandon ship, jettison children, cats, houses, bills. Ship to shore. Ship out. On the way, the ganglia of back roads leading north were filled with tiger lilies.

What I have thought was avoidance was to deny—what? When you told me the day we had drinks—the second meeting that led to the third, an hour in which crucial information was exchanged between us—we proceeded from there: everything that happened between us up to the moment we decided to part was based on that knowledge. It was left unresolved. Beauty walks a razor's edge. I trusted you from the beginning, you said. That was a mistake. And I thought, why is he telling me this? And my refusal to trust you—why is that? That I can think you will forget me in a week, a day? So that I can walk away? When the children were little, I read them the story of the Snow Queen, a tale in which the ending takes a long time to happen, a story unfolding inside another, an origami snowflake that holds another snowflake, and another, like the Morton Salt girl who retreats into a speck of salt. The first rule of fantasy is—do not break the rules: Tinkerbell will die, she can't not die, no matter how much you might want her to live; the marble boy gets one hour a year, not more; Orpheus, my darling, must not turn to look at Eurydice. But what kind of person doesn't look back? For a lost glove, a hat, a child? In his journal, the blue crosshatched pattern on the cover blurred by rain, Michael wrote: *I even wrote to Patsy that at this point I really have no idea exactly what our trip* will be like, or what will happen; one moment I'm filled with a feeling of inadequacy, the next I am full of excitement.

A story about a man who was lost. A feeling of not being up to it, just now. The week before we parted, you told me a little story about Henry, a toddler in your building. One afternoon Henry was with his father in the lobby; you picked him up to play with him, and he began to suck a button on your shirt, and would not let go. He latched on to it, and rolled it around in his mouth, his nose in your chest. It was a way of making love, of finding in that button everything he liked about you, and wanted, not only from you but from the universe. When I saw the boxer, it was all I could do not to touch his mottled skin, as the baby put your button in his mouth. Every place on his body was a map of injury. The statue was buried in order to preserve it. And then it was found? Yes, that is what you told me. A man who was hurt and lost and disappeared and then was rescued? Yes. That is what he is.

What else is buried in order to be preserved? Injury. But the whole idea of preservation, impossible. Boiling the fruit, the scalded jars, the little rubber rings. No, even I know I am too careless for that, a crone serving up a sugary treat, the company dead in a week. Vanessa Bell said, I feel that I am always the youngest person in the omnibus. What age are you?—a question at dinner a week ago. For years I said, nineteen. It was the year I met Alastair. What is the truth, still? Is it the truth that I have never loved anyone the way I love Alastair? Or loved Alastair. It makes no difference, really. As you have told me, it doesn't matter what you say today or tomorrow. When I think of him now, he is on the sofa, weeping, his back heaving. Was it bare? It doesn't matter. I know Alastair's back like the back of my hand, the arch of my foot. In the bathroom, bent at the waist, Alastair looked in the mirror, and two clouds of condensation bloomed on the glass. I take myself to task, I say, it is so long ago, can't you see you are repeating yourself; you are writing a long letter, but your whole life has been a long letter, addressed to god knows who: the man in the moon, the tiny people who live in the radio, singing jingles, the fat lady on the dock in North Haven. I can see you shaking your head. I wonder if this should be addressed to you at all; you are not an unreliable narrator but an unreliable listener. And you behave like a child, always needing someone to pay attention. If I turn away, message after message arrives that says, I know nothing but that I love you. The worst kind of manipulation; nothing ever changes. Yes, but it can stop and start. You said, I do not want you to be the next thing. But something is always next, yes?

Because the hardest thing to realize is that one is forgettable, and perhaps that is one of the lessons you set yourself out to teach me, though never "on purpose," or with premeditation: that everyone can be reduced to someone who has been forgotten. Shutters close over the valley, where a woman limps up and down to Santa Maria di Lignano, where at night wild boars eat the dark. One is left with oneself, someone for whom simply not having to put her head in a Food Fair bag is enough of an accomplishment for a morning. A woman who has let go of a timetable, whose youngest child still cleaves to her side as she passes through the country of the enemy, a cross-stich map that she has made herself. A woman who has inherited a tablecloth embroidered by her aunt, her grandmother, and her great-grandmother, a hedge of green stiches turned into flowers. A woman who was a girl, drawn by a spirograph, each story a circle, a way into a labyrinth that proved to be not a labyrinth but a maze. When

I first spoke to Alastair after twenty-three or twenty-eight years, how many was it, a forest had grown up between us, and only by entering that forest could we find—what? It was snowing then, in the mirror. A story I have told you. Tell me, you said. This morning on the cove I woke up from a dream, skipped a bottom stair, and hurled into space, as in those early years living with Alastair I imagined throwing myself off the roof. Shall I tell it as you would tell a story? When I first came to New York, I had a love affair with a woman I met on a bus, who lived on —— Street. I did not meet Alastair on a bus. Instead of your *it was complicated, but it lasted only a brief time*, we can substitute: *it was complicated, and it went on and on*. When Alastair read the account of that story, he wrote to me that what confounded him most was kindness. Whose? I asked. Sometimes I feel there are two Carolines, one who understands making your bed and lying in it, and the other who lies in that bed and has bad dreams, which she cuts out herself with nail scissors. You do not want them; you have enough bad dreams. And I cannot give them to Frank, precisely because he wants them. There is no such thing for me as a two-way street. The children tell me to sit down, they can't talk to me when I am circling, I never pay any attention, there is no use talking to me. I come upstairs and I think, what am I doing here? What did I forget? The other evening, now it is much later, in another life, I was taken to meet a woman in a beautiful empty apartment in the West Village. Almost nothing in it: an African mask, a leather chair. She is ninety. She told me they say the old have time, and I thought that, too, the days with so little to fill them. But time now moves so quickly.

With trigger sureness, everything confounds me. I want, you said, as we sat in the garden full of white flowers, to be wholly available to you. It is the last thing you want. Louie and

Pom are in the kitchen. We have driven back from camp, with her lanyards and tennis racquet. You have called during dinner to say you will not be available until Tuesday, you will call me later, you will write with times that you might be able to get free over the weekend; you do not call later and you do not write. And I do not say, but I am not free this weekend, the children are here, Louie leaves for her summer job tomorrow and I have to take them to the movies, Pom has lost her bathing suit and Dinda is here overnight, and Monday I must run around the city with Pom to replace what she has lost at camp before we leave next week. The hydrangeas are drooping in the garden. I let you think that you are not seeing me . . . but that I am waiting for you. Why do I do this? Because I would perhaps switch the hours around, let the children go to the movies themselves? But—I do not write or call. As I type I know that none of these words really count—the scenario unfolds in a puppet theater made from a shoebox. A phantasm. Yesterday I went to see Victor. Instead of his office downtown, he had me come to his apartment on Ninety-Eighth Street. A large apartment, in which the seventies furnishings are frozen in place. The low, linen-covered sofa, the farmhouse table, the interesting objects, the Miró lithograph. An apartment one has been in a hundred times before, except that it is scrupulously clean, scrubbed down and vacuumed. The sun was hitting the sofa, and there were no dust motes. Was it only yesterday? But I couldn't find the building. I was downtown, and when I came up at Ninety-Sixth Street, the map had shifted. I could not remember which way the numbers went on Ninety-Eighth Street, in the city where I have lived almost all my life. A woman wanted me to sign a petition for city council; I told her I could not because I knew nothing about the special election, an admission that made me feel, in the face of her ardent delivery, her dedication to the Upper West Side, like a flibbertigibbet, a person of no character, unable to find an address on a street on which she has found herself perhaps one thousand times. I think—I know—that I was disconcerted because it is Esther's neighborhood, but I did not know her address. As I walked back and forth across Broadway, there was a man on the traffic island, with a bunch of flowers wrapped in white paper. It was a large bouquet of sunflowers and roses, exactly like the bouquet I had bought for a dinner party the night before and put on the piano, so like it that my first thought was, why does this man have my flowers? The man was holding the flowers oddly, above his head, as if he were trying the hail a taxi with the bouquet. From the back he looked exactly like you, his hair cut exactly like yours at the nape. I was on the west side of Broadway, and the light changed—and he crossed quickly (so he was not hailing a taxi, after all) and sped east on Ninety-Eighth Street, and disappeared under the awning of the first building on the corner, which was obscured by a moving van. It was very hot. Sun glinted in the mica on the sidewalk. I had it in my mind that I was looking for number 200, and when I followed the man who was carrying my flowers, I saw that the building number was 225. I realized, 200 is across the street. So I went back, avoiding the lady with the petition, crossing to the north side of Ninety-Eighth Street so I would not have to say "That kind of day," or "Looking for an address," some banality to inform her that though I looked mad, I was not, although by now it was clear to me and perhaps to her, a nice, earnest lady who wanted me to endorse so-and-so, who had been endorsed by Michael Moore, the filmmaker, for city council, that I had lost my mind, and then went back across Broadway and looked at the list of names at 200 to see if Esther's name was there. It was not. I then thought to look at the note I'd made on my phone—quite laboriously, using the Notes feature for the first time—and saw that Victor's building was west, not east, on Ninety-Eighth Street, toward West End Avenue. There was a man with dreadlocks and a briefcase, and a bored teenager with an old, sad black dog, whose tank top read LOVE in different colors, waiting for the elevator. When the door opened, a woman with a black braid wearing what we used to call a peasant skirt, propelling a stroller, rammed into me, and gave me a look that meant, I have a stroller and I have the right of way, and I felt myself turned around six times in what had become, unaccountably, a maze of streets, losing my temper. But I did not say to her: I spent more than a decade of my life pushing strollers in and out of elevators; it is your fault, not mine, that you are not paying attention to where you are going, and your life, too, may turn out not exactly as you expected; one day you may be standing outside an apartment building in which someone you love is carrying your flowers to give to someone else. But I knew, you see, that it was a hallucination—you, and the flowers. Because it was not you; you were somewhere else entirely. And then I went up and sat on the white couch under the Miró print and the mandalas, and I did not tell Victor about the hallucination. I told him about my trip to Maine, and he said, the problem is when metaphors become symptoms.

Finally, you have extricated yourself, and we go to see a play by an old friend, or friend of a friend, or son of a friend— a play about cats. When we left the theater it was impossible to get a taxi; Lafayette Street was dark, and it felt for a moment like SoHo in the seventies, when we drifted on the cobblestones like shadows of shadows. Do you feel like that, you said, that I am annihilating you? Was that a line in the play? I cannot remember who said what, but as you constantly remind me, it doesn't matter who says what. There are two kinds of anxieties, Victor says: engulfment and abandonment. Abandonment I know; it is my old friend, carrying a Coach bag, with a streak of pure white at her brow. On one hand, abandonment, wearing a pear-shaped diamond; on the other, engulfment, a raised hand. The left does not know what the right is doing, the enemy of my friend is my enemy, but the friend of my enemy is also my enemy. Last night, I slept for hours in your room like a seashell, and now type at the parquet table, wearing your white undershirt, while you have gone who knows where, the air conditioner full blast, before I go downtown. I have made myself coffee in a large mug. What are we fastidious about? Kindness. Loyalty. Holding two thoughts at the same time. Prevarication as a kind of truth. Of a kind. The phrase *We cannot go on* is written in shaving cream on the mirror. But we can. A little while. I said at dinner at Café Alzette, with that ridiculous waiter who thinks he is in an episode of *The Love Boat*, that I had two things to say—one is about Pom, the other, a story. The difference between you is that you do not ask for the story. You wait. Below the window a man walks by playing the banjo. Just pickle my bones in alcohol. In the Asmat's drawings, a stick figure can be a man, or a mantis. Count the fingers. The first entry of the Chronological Report of Searching Activities of Drowning Person in the Agats Area—November 1961, reads:

> The villagers in Agats told us that a Catamarran had capsized with three white men, maybe drowned near the Eilander river mouth. This reached the Commando post (Meruke). Administration officer (HPAB Agats) took a motorboat to Duorga. There was a request to ask the Tasman vessel (in the neighborhood of Jamas) to try to approach the site of the capsizing ASAP.

From the governor's remarks at Idlewild Airport, November 29, 1961:

I would just like to say a word about Michael himself. Ever since he was little, he has been very aware of people, their feelings, their thoughts . . . He is a person who has always loved people and has always been loved by people. He has always loved beauty . . . He had made the trip before, the trip he was taking when the accident occurred. It is something that can happen.

Here is a story about Pom. What kind of an animal would you be if you could come back as an animal? But I did, I did. What kind of animal? An ocelot. A smoking-mirror monster-killer. But if the mirror was full of smoke, how could you see yourself in it? The mirror wasn't full of smoke, it was *made* of smoke. When Tezcatlipoca was cast down from the sky by Quetzalcoatl, he fell into the river and then rose up as an ocelot and slew the monsters. Ocelots hunt near water. Sometimes he wears a crown of feathers. Who? Tezcatlipoca. He is missing a foot, but it doesn't matter because he has a foot of obsidian; his foot mirrors the ground. The mirror of smoke? Yes. For school, this spring, she made a diorama of the river, and an overhanging tree, and a smoky mirror. The smoke is cotton wool. And there is a little glass rooster so that the ocelot will have something to eat. Poor rooster. At the Aztec festival Pom wore a headdress of feathers. What do you see when you look in the mirror? Smoke. A small old-fashioned boy, reading *Dombey and Son*, in love with his sister. In the apartment of stories, when my cousins and I tired of magic tricks, of trying to bend spoons, we played the animal game. You lived upstairs. Last week you said, your skin is terrible, running your hand along my calf, puckered by small patches of eczema. It is because you make the shower too hot, you said. And then you said, about Stefano, under the steam, I am too hard on him. I am rarely hard on Pom; it is she who is hard on me. They all are—they want my attention with the mania of collectors. You do not; you would rather be a cat, or a constellation, constant in the darkness. You opened the glass door of the shower and went to shave at the sink, which has now reappeared like a sink in a Duchamp painting. You said, what is it? The steam was smoke on the mirror. And I heard my voice, a lifetime ago, saying, "Don't show off" in the bathroom with Alastair on Eighty-Fourth Street, as I came up from behind, naked, and put my arms around him. An aperçu, a tiny dart. A flinch. We were twenty-four, twenty-six. Even early in the morning he smelled of gin. In the mirror, you in your black-and-white bathrobe, you said, there was a story you didn't finish telling me.

Yesterday, the morning I went downstairs after making the bed and put some laundry in, watered the garden, and finally unpacked the suitcase that I had taken to Maine. Though why, I don't know, we are leaving for the rest of the summer on Saturday. I was thinking, as I threw out the shriveled lemons from the vegetable bin, here I am doing necessary tasks. How orderly I am! Ridiculous. Louie and Pom were asleep upstairs. And then, the feeling it is a charade, I am a fraud, I want to put my head in the laundry basket and weep. In the house where I was a child there was a small casement window in the closet, and when I was perhaps thirteen I would shut myself in the closet and look out at the peaked roof over the porch. The ivy climbed over the dormer; I trained it to come in through the window, and I pretended to be Sleeping Beauty in her bower, but even then I knew that I wasn't a beauty; I was a monster. I can hear you saying, "Who taught you that?" and then, but it is better to be *una monstra!* Because a monster is turned inside out! The moon lit the tulip tree, and the tree tossed down its fleshy blooms. I pretended to be a changeling; across the terraced lawn was a wing of the castle in which I was hidden. A banal dream. Was it the not-here that propelled me? And you would say, it is always nice to be elsewhere, and you know it, too, going here, there, everywhere in your falling-apart car. At that age I was in thrall to a boy called Jeremy, who smelled of peppermints. He lived with his mother and his brother, Harry, who beat him up, in a huge house about a mile away. His father had left. This was still novel. His mother did not get out of bed, some days. She had platinum-blond hair and was called Baby by everyone, including her children. The housekeeper was called Tati. Like Olivia, who worked for Alastair's mother, Tati was from Jamaica, from a place called Cassava Piece. Tati often said to Jeremy, "Sweetie, you would not last a minute in Cassava Piece, they would take the bejesus right out of you." Sometimes Jeremy muttered under his breath as he put his hand inside my jeans, "I'm going to take the bejesus right out of you." What was the bejesus? Where? Jeremy was a year older, he had already had a girlfriend. Her name was Lara; she had an identical twin sister, and her brother was in jail for heroin possession. It was 1973.

It is like a rotating stage in a theater, but you always say no when I say it is as if I arrived in the mezzanine a little early and I am holding your place for you so we can sit together. You do not view life as a series of dramatic episodes, in which the scenes that will happen are as vivid as the ones that have occurred. For you there is only the past and now. A Japanese fan can open, a little wand, or a pointer, but for now it is closed. How sure I have been, how certain, to say that I would not be a woman waiting in the doorway under the hive of golden light, across from the Naturalists Gate. But perhaps that is what I am. Is that the truth of it? What is the story you tell about me?

Do you remember the day before I left, you said to me, *vuoi vino, tè, o acqua minerale?* And I said water. You asked for tea, and when the waiter brought it, I asked you if you wanted sugar, and you said, unusually for you, that you already had your sugar. I had brought you lacecap hydrangeas from the garden. The palazzo is closed for the season or not yet open, although I am peering as one does through the shutters, standing on tiptoe, my skirt and hands will be dusty, and you will say, wash your hands. Today at the fishmonger with Frank, who keeps his hand on my waist as if I were about to slip away, although I am here with him, as you are wherever you are, with Esther, there was a fat baby in a pram whose name was Stefano. At the restaurant you said, about Pom, what do I say, I love your mother, put up with it? But she *likes* you, I said. I do not want something next, you said, I want something new. I am reading Dorothy Sayers before bed, the fan going. Frank says he woke at three and there were fireflies in the trees; the light was so strong it woke him. Wake me, I said, so I can see it. He does not wake me, because he is now sleeping through the night, as if a burden were lifted, despite the medicine that makes him sick, and means he cannot go out in the sun, his beautiful seventeenth-century face turned from me. I wake instead and get up and turn on the fan. In the afternoon it's ninety degrees at six p.m.; we sit on the glider on the porch, covered with wisteria, drinking vodka with ice which melts immediately. Even the mosquitoes have heatstroke and do not bother us. He is angry with me.

There are too many scenes I'd like to have skipped and did not. I remember shopping with my mother when I was a child, the crinolines endlessly repeated in the shop mirrors, a paper-doll chain of Carolines. Was one different from another?

I wanted to be the Caroline farthest away. So many fix-it stories. I read the children *The Tailor of Gloucester*, with his tiny thread, *The Snow Queen*, with Kai's shattered sled. The day I saw the bloodied boxer at the museum, afterward, I went to see *L'Avventura*, at the Metrograph. At two in the afternoon, there were three people in the theater. Yes, you told me to see it, too. Monica Vitti, in a polka-dot dress, goes to see a man, whose name is Sandro. They take a cruise with some friends; on an island where they stop to swim she disappears. And then within a few minutes, *presto*, Sandro falls in love with her friend, Claudia.

> CLAUDIA: Why did you come?
> SANDRO: I couldn't help it.
> CLAUDIA: Well, we'll have to help it, so you might as well make this sacrifice right now.

---

*A goshawk flies over the maze. A double mirror, the maze reflected in the goshawk's eye, the child now at a distance of time looking back at herself, in a smocked white dress in the declivity by the boxwood. It is summer, the white hydrangea blossoms drum the air. "Carnation, lily, lily, rose, have you seen my Flora pass this way?" She is a girl in a white dress painted by Sargent, holding a magic lantern, a lantern slide doubled back in the mirror. The eye of the goshawk is the oculus mundi, the earth a green-and-gold iris bound by the white orbital bone. Distance is measured by the number of vertices between two points. In 1646, on page 28 of* Ars Magna Lucis et Umbrae, *Athanasius Kircher, polymath, drew a contraption of two mirrors, which opened like a book, depicting the reflection of doubled polygon figures. In Mechanick Exercises (1684), the printer Joseph Moxon wrote describing the wooden printers' box:*

That the Partitions lye close to the bottom of the Case, that so the Letters slide not through an upper into an under Box, when the Papers of the Boxes may be worn.

His note: "Regulæ Trium Ordinum Literarum Typographicarum; or the Rules of the Three Orders of Print Letters, viz: the Roman, Italick, English; By Joseph Moxon, Hydrographer to the King's Most Excellent Majesty. Printed for Joseph Moxon on Ludgate Hill, at the Sign of Atlas, 1676."

The field tilts as the goshawk tilts his head. She keeps her balance by standing on one foot. "Oh dear! Oh dear! I shall be too late!" said the rabbit. And Alice fortunately "was just in time to see it pop down a large rabbit-hole under the hedge." If she turns around in the boxwood hedge, there is another door and another. But what time is it? Hurry up, please. It had begun with the letter A, and she had hoisted herself up, hand over hand, and now she stood holding the mast of the letter P, the sail billowing. Tick-tock. Curiosity killed the cat, says the tell-tale. For a Brownie campfire badge, the requirements are Discover, Take Action, Connect. Roll a newspaper into sticks. In one square, Pascal, thin as an airmail letter. What is the best place to put a mast on a ship? In his first entry to the Académie royale des sciences de Paris, Euler took second place. He was thirteen. The lord giveth and the lord taketh away. A thunderhead over the boxwood, a hand drawing a charcoal cloud with enormous force, the stick splintering to smithereens. In each square: death by water, death by fire. "I am having the most wonderful and interesting time," wrote Michael Rockefeller to his father, the governor. Roll back the ball, sweetheart. How will she stand it, in her white smocked dress in the vestibule, when even now the charcoal cloud is rolling overhead, drawn by someone whom she will love much later, when she is old, whom she loves now but does not know it, who—just now as she stands in the boxwood—is a boy drawing a train crossing the prairie, the noise deafening. He cannot keep away from it, the past's dark dust. A game of snakes and ladders. With his penknife, he whittles the roots of the locust tree. Who is he when he's at home? The doors are locked, she cannot open them. It is summer—the hot day makes her sleepy and stupid—but if she closes her eyes, she is a girl inside a snow globe, standing by the ball fields. A boy kicks a ball, he is playing kickball although it is snowing, and when it lands by her feet, she kicks it back. She is freezing. Roll the ball back, sweetheart. A bouncing game. A, my name is Alastair, and I sell apples. Her first love. His name is the letter A; here he is, under the eave, curled in a ball on the branch of a locust tree. What could she have been thinking? In the fairy tale inside the snow globe, she lifts the latch. In this square it is snowing in the boxwood. If she looks into the high-peaked room, a double mirror. Or is it doubled vision, seen through tears? The room is very cold. Why do you always wear a belt? he asks, and takes the belt off, slithering it through the belt loops, holding the tooth of the buckle in his hand. The snaking cord connecting the screen to the electric socket is a white mouse tail; on the screen is a film she has told him she cannot watch. That is the impasse between them; she cannot watch. He has described it to her, a woman with her back cut in a checkerboard, another. Stop. Go back. In the vestibule in the boxwood she cannot think. It is impossible for her to buckle her own shoes, the shoes marked with the letter A; other children have shoes with laces, why can't she? If she curls up very tight, she can fit herself inside the letter hoops, Moxon's Capitals and Smalls, Compounded of Geometrick Figures, and mostly made by Rule and Compass. Her throat closes. Here she is inside a C, for Caroline. Dear-line. The letter is the same whether it is big or small. Pie in the sky, an irrational number. The smell of burning is very near; in the playground a boy holding a magnifying glass lit a beetle on fire. Distances are measured by the number of vertices. Her mind flips, one thing after another. Her heart is a pump. Each leaf is a tongue. Only you, says the bear, *only you can prevent forest fires*. It was a long time ago. The hedge is full of charcoal dust from the drawings of thunderheads. It settles on her shoes, on the white bull's head, sifting down on each square of the maze. He said, Miss Mouse, will you marry me? Not for all the salt in the deep blue sea, uh-huh. Above, the goshawk's eye opens then shuts. She shifts from foot to foot. Each square is at the center of the maze; each one is superimposed on the other. Each bridge is a line connecting one swale to another. The sound of a charcoal stick on paper. In 1828, twelve-year-old Ada Lovelace considered paper, wire, and oilskin as possible materials for wings. Also feathers. The maze tilts. On the dock below the boxwood hedge, she is just learning to walk. Come, Caroline, her mother says. She is wearing a white dress smocked with pink; her mother holds her arms out to her (it is impossible to see her mother clearly, the piercing light cannot find her; her mother in a shadow holds her arms out to her); but it is the letter V, and she veers away, and unless she is stopped or falls, she will step out into thin air over the water. *Fear no more the heat o' the sun, nor the furious winter's rages.* The film is black-and-white, you cannot see the pink thread. And, or, not. A long arm grabs her and obscures the camera lens. She is stopped. A drone of bees. Move the mouse. She stands very still in the boxwood, the litter of letters at her feet.

◦

*Bene, dovremo aiutarlo, quindi vale tanto fare questo sacrificio in questo momento*. A mise-en-scène, as opposed to a *mise en abyme*, is not complete without narration. Yes. Tell me what you are thinking about this morning. I am thinking about you. I am not sure, by the way, that it is exactly me you are thinking about. And these paragraphs are a way to talk to me when we are not speaking? Yes. That is how they started, and how they have gone on. Because there are many ways in which we do not speak. I want to get to the end. When will that be, do you think? In the fall, I imagine. Which is soon. Soon is always sooner for you than for me. After six months you said, this is very new. To me it wasn't so new then. But it was getting old the way it was, yes? Yes. But it was you who had set all these parameters: once a month for thirty years. I know. But I didn't know what it was. Perhaps it is nothing. Perhaps, but you will have gotten all these pages out of it. Which for you may be the most important thing, anyway. I do not want that to be the most important: I want everything to be important. *Sì, sei avida. Non si può avere tutto, tesoro. Hai mica pensato a mè quando sei andata ad East Hampton?* Yes. I missed you most when in the taxi I passed the Waldbaum's where we bought milk. The Waldbaum's? Yes. We'd never been to a market together. Well, at least you are teaching yourself Italian. Though who is teaching you, I don't know—the syntax is terrible. Your mother spoke terrible Italian. She did not! She spoke perfect Italian, terribly.

The next day, I am back in Mattapoisett. I walk to the beach, and when I return, I make coffee in the impossible kitchen. It is taking too long. I reach for the pot while it is still dripping. The coffee sizzles. And there is your voice again when I am not listening for it: you are impatient and you make a mess. Is that what this is all about? My impatience? But I am tired of the catch in my throat. You mean you must stop being in love with me to love me again? Yes. But you may not be able to do that. Don't give yourself airs. At least not so many. Louie comes into the kitchen. She wants to know if I have ever been to a strip club. There are turkeys on the lawn; I think they are nesting under the house. And two days ago, with Frank, we saw a fin in the water. I wonder what else I have forgotten. To you, this house exists in the fold of a Japanese fan, accessible only by boat, or a passage out of time, navigated by the spirits of the dead, who are always moving between the past and the present, a place where language disappears, A, or B, it does not matter. When I was a child, we played a terrible game. What was it? You could play with two or three or four people. One person thought of a word; on a sheet of paper, or a blackboard. For each letter you put a dash. Each person guessed a letter. Five, six, seven. Longer words were better. After two or three letters, often people began to guess the word and fill in the letters. The person who announced the last letter won. But the terrible thing was that as you guessed the letters, you also drew a little stick figure, one line for each wrong guess: a leg, an arm. The goal was to guess the word before you drew the figure; if you did not, you drew a noose around the head of the stick figure. It was called hangman. If you could not guess the right letters, the little stick figure was hanged. How can it be that we played such a horrible game? The letters flinched. In the United States, in 1965 or '6 or '7? It was a spelling game. We played it in the car, when we were bored; we played it at school on the blackboard. Let's play hangman!

It did not occur to anyone that this game was terrible. I could not bear it, the little chalky head, the little chalk noose, the consequences of guessing the right word. Later, I looked it up: the game was first recorded in Britain, in 1884, in a book called *Birds, Beasts, and Fishes*. By 1902 it was popular in America at meetings of the Vigilance Society, where members "wore white caps and masks." How can we have played this? We did. This morning, the day heating up, midges in the locusts. If you are not here, I need to learn to speak without you. But you could have come. No, I could not. And you did not invite me. That was because you would not come, and I could not bear to hear you say it. I know that, but what I know is that one by one, you send people away. At first they do not know they are being sent away, but then they do know, and they are gone.

Pom is downstairs now, making a kite out of newspaper on the dining room table. Up, up, up it will go, from the high dune down the road. She is making a tail out of leftover pink and green birthday ribbons. It won't fly, says Louie, who is ignored, then offers to paint it with clouds. She goes to find her watercolor box. Pom says, why doesn't she make her own kite? Why does everyone always *get in the way*? When I read a page of this letter aloud to you, you said, about Esther, do you have to use her real name? Yes, I said. Is that wise, you asked—*ma solo si può dire. You* and *yes* are the same word? Yes. Rhyme's desperate measures. Pom wants to measure our hands. Palms together. Her hands are already a little bigger than mine. Here is the church, here is the steeple. She is writing a novel. I imagine Stefano has not written a novel. Of course not. Lucky him. I see we are speaking. Perhaps it is best, to unravel a bit your voice in my head. The August chill is coming on. Later on she balls up the leftover newspaper to make a fire in the grate. The warped shutters on the windows are inside the house, not out: Indian shutters, to keep out Indians. Mama, you can't say *Indian*, says Louie. Roll it back, sweetheart, I hear Daniel say, drifting downstream on a leaf.

What were Daniel's parents' names? Moshe and Goldie. My parents met at Treblinka, is what he always said, with an ironic laugh and grimace. It's a boy-meets-girl story, yes? And then a shrug, a wave of the hand, the palm arcing backward to say, who cares? Enough already. *Basta.* He liked to speak Italian, short phrases. He admired the working classes and aspired to be a carpenter, a house painter. A man with his education! his father-in-law said. As I type I am imagining what it would have been like in bed with Daniel. Then, it did not cross my mind. A man holding a baby while my stomach is pumped, who wiped my brow with a red bandana. Later, he began to spend money, a set of the most expensive golf clubs in the world, made of a special kind of wood, although he did not play golf, as though he was trying to hit a ball into another world. Just write: he lost his mind. A few minutes have elapsed. To stop thinking about this, I have gone downstairs to fold the beach towels. What is the effect of tyranny when you are small? As a child? Is my inability to look at tyranny tied to my insistence that it is time to think about other things? Finally, to believe that whatever happened, it could have been worse. It is worse, at every moment, at every longitude and latitude, a net of barbed wire. Take a stand, said the man on the way to a hanging. As James notes in his preface to *The Ambassadors*, "There is the story of one's hero, and then, thanks to the intimate connexion of things, the story of one's story itself"; and, then, "The 'first person' then, so employed, is addressed by the author directly to ourselves." A crossword. But never a cross word. If you don't have something nice to say, keep it to yourself. Are you listening, Caroline? You can't catch flies with vinegar. You don't know how to talk to people you don't like. Don't love, really. Turn the page. Each black book bound to the wall. A feeling of inadequacy. It is something that can happen. For Michael, what was the alternative? In Connecticut, in New York, in Cambridge? He swam toward shore, buoyed by two oil cans. From John D. Rockefeller, Jr: *Dear Michael, I am happy to have the wooden birdhouse you made all by yourself. It arrived today. It is a very nice birthday present.*

A twister picked him up. The hospital room was the last place I saw Daniel. That is, I saw him here and there, the following day, after I had recovered and spent the afternoon lying down in an upstairs room at their house in Tulsa, a room as usual so untidy and brazenly filthy that it was hard to rest, so strong was the impulse to sweep it clean, the blankets, the sheets, the molting armchair. But we did not speak again. I think I drove myself to the airport. Daniel put the baby in the car seat, I do remember that. It was that period when we rented car seats and bought juice boxes and always had something in our pockets for babies to play with. It was the last time I saw him, then, when he put Pom in the car.

It was April. By July that year a twister had lifted Daniel up. It did not set him down. He left Tulsa. He bought four hundred acres of land in Arizona and pitched a tent. He spoke on street corners. He had always been able to talk for a long time about the Spanish Civil War. Now he did not stop. It was not particularly easy to befriend junkies in Tulsa, but the ones who were still alive became his best friends. He returned home at five in the morning. Then he did not return for days. He had a cassette tape of *Bringing It All Back Home*, and he played it until it broke. Kettledrums and flypaper. That was what was playing in the car when he came back and tried to pick up Izzy and Max from school in the Maserati. Here's a sentence for you: Daniel was carrying a machete in the back of the Maserati. The long *ee* sounds high, pitched—carry, machete, Maserati, a shriek under the sentence, like a train grinding gears, or worse, a train, its windows sealed, headed for the oven.

There was an abandoned chicken coop on the property. The house next to it had fallen down. He moved into it. There were a lot of old magazines in the chicken coop, a rocking chair, blankets on the floor. He was going to recycle the magazines, but there was an article in one he wanted. The chicken coop was not heated; magazines provided insulation. A babel of words. I don't know what he did for money—odd jobs. Perhaps there was an allowance administered by the sausage factory. Izzy and Max drove out to see him. By then Izzy could drive. She hadn't seen her father in two years. It was cold but not snowing. He had bought them sandwiches for lunch. They played Risk. He had two beers, and his jokes were funny. He gave them math problems, the Hadwiger conjecture, Mother's worm problem: what is the region of smallest area that can contain every planar arc of length, an arc of length being something that "locally looks like a line." His eyes were black under his thick brows which were now two caterpillars threaded with silver. They had stayed in a motel nearby, and drove back to Tulsa the next day. They said it was a good visit. The next day I received an email which said, *Call for terrible news.* It was Boxing Day. In New York the snow was falling so hard that you could not see out the big window in the living room; there were six inches of snow on the table in the garden. The fire started in the gas stove. The magazines added to the heat of the blaze.

Roll back the ball, sweetheart. The morning we left the hospital he said, I thought when I saw you, you would die there in the ICU, and that she would be mine, another baby. Thirteen years later in the kitchen in New York the baby who is now thirteen hates cauliflower. It gives her a stomachache. You don't like it either, she says, and you don't like broccoli. I do like broccoli, I say, but I can't eat it. She wants to know why. Because when my appendix was taken out when you were a baby, it left some scar tissue. I can't eat broccoli. How do you know? I know, I say. I tell her about the hospital in the middle of the night, and how she came with me and tore up magazines. You were tiny, I say. She listens, her pencil down. She is doing her math homework while I make supper. Daniel took care of me? she asks. Yes. I tell her more about the magazines, how she ripped up so many the floor was covered. Newsprint isn't good for babies, she says. I shrug. She giggles: I am notorious for feeding small children oysters and strawberries. Peanuts. A war on the idea of risk. When they were teething, I put whisky on their gums. What happened to him? To whom? I ask. Do you remember him? It is a stupid question; she was eight months old, of course she does not remember him. She barely remembers Naomi, who swoops in from time to time for an hour or two on her way somewhere else. The truce between us edgy. We do not see, as they say, eye to eye. It doesn't matter. If you are on fire, roll yourself in a blanket so the flames do not spread, so that your stockings do not catch on fire. The flames spread. Like marimba music, the gas flame under the minestrone. It is past suppertime; she came home late from a softball game. Why do you say "what happened?" I ask. She doesn't bother to answer me. I am being fatuous. She is almost thirteen.

What happened to him? Her blue eyes the color of the gas jet. When her great-grandmother was little, she hid in a closet, she hid under a bed. A little girl whose own mother washed her in a tub of milk to keep her skin soft. I do the calculations. If she were ten, I would not tell her. I turn down the minestrone which is sticking a little to the bottom of the pot, and sit down at the table. There is a bowl of fruit on the table, two mangos, a Bosc pear which should be thrown out, and two bananas.

I go far, far back, so she will understand the story. I tell her about Daniel in high school, how he was good at math, how good he was at getting a parking space. This is a magic she respects. What else can I tell her? I explain a little about bipolar disorder: she knows about bipolar disorder; she had a unit in school on diseases of the brain. She knows everything about it, and I know nothing. You get it in your twenties, not when you are old, she says. He couldn't have had it. I tell her he began to spend money and be a little scary, but I do not tell her about the machete. How was he scary. I tell her about the machete. As I speak I wonder why I am telling her this. *Kein ayin hora*, my grandmother would say. Because rather than shielding my children, I want them to be wary? Or this child, to whom I have said things I would cut off my hand not to have said. As if that would do any good. A wish. Wish: to want, hope for, crave, hanker after. I wished him farewell: to bid. Fear no more the lightning flash. How to make a wish? Out of what? Consign to thee, the air leaving the body, blowing out candles, a dandelion's frowzy head, as if the spirit filled that thing desired. For a wish is an admission that something is lacking.

I tell her the story I have told you, here. But then I wanted to tell you, about why I was crying in the car, on my way here to the Cape. Oh please, enough, *basta*, I can hear you say. I was crying about Daniel, I was crying about telling lies, and about wanting and not wanting to call you from the car, and wanting to call one or two other people as well, whom I also did not call, because I've read the fine print; the statute of limitations on certain kinds of phone calls has worn out. You must stop, said Alida, at ninety, as we walk down the sandy path to Crow Beach. You must stop seeing Lorenzo. It is unbecoming.

We will return to the city in a week; the beach grass is turning gold on the verge by the inlet. The hedge is bejeweled with rose hips. The children will go back to school; I will find Pom's school skirt, and it will be too small for her. I am afraid that when I get back to New York and walk through the door, you will take my hands and place them by my sides, and it will be over. I will wake up from the dream. I know you think that. What did the rude mechanicals want? Who? In the parking lot, when you went to Maine to visit Alastair. They wanted to help. They wanted to help? I looked like a person in need of assistance. Mustardseed grows up to be Titania; there is always a slot for the Fairy Queen. And for cabbages and kings. That is always true. Were the rude mechanicals real? They appeared in the parking lot. It wasn't late summer; it was snowing. It is still snowing, there at that moment in the parking lot. But they were not wearing coats. Yes. No.

But not everyone wears a coat when it is snowing; in the story of the Snow Queen, Kai did not wear a coat, and Gerda searched for him, up and down and across, in the smallest region that can be measured on the lines of a planar curve. There was ice on the windshield. There were parts of the pond that weren't frozen; there had been a thaw, and moonlit pockets where the reflections of the pine trees skated upside down on the water. Pines, not nutmeg trees. There was a canoe on the bank covered with snow, the hull like Swiss cheese, a remark made by Alastair's grandfather; a canoe that has taken on water for forty years. An owl in the branches above the pond. Or an ocelot. Part of that story I told you opens only now, years later, when it is hot and still, and the fan unfolds to stir the air. The blanket in the back of the car was moth-eaten; last night we took it to the top of the dune to see the Pleiades. Was it the same blanket? What did the stars look like at night, on the Asmat river? I'll swim to shore, he said. In the house where we are now the windows behind the shutters are Sandwich glass. And? And. The box hedge by the drive is full of bees; the grapes are just starting in the arbor; a mile away at night you can hear the ocean. There is a whippoorwill in the garden. Is the ocelot far from home? He is far from home. On the road I see myself coming and going. Seven maids with seven mops could not sweep it all up, if they swept for half a year. I am just telling you. I know you are not interested in Sandwich glass.

There are many things we cannot think about, so we think about them *attorno ai bordi*. It is better? I think. Is the language coming more naturally to you, now? Yes. Then it will be yours. It is not Linear A or B, it is a later language. We can go again, to Todi, or you will go. We will decide what is best. What did you read, when you could not sleep last night? Montale. Which poems? The book keeps opening at "The House by the Sea." How does it start? *Il viaggio finisce qui. E più tardi?* Yes. I can't remember if you dislike early or late Montale. Late. This is the middle. Yes, I know. There is also the poem to Liuba:

> *La casa che tuc rechi*
> *con te ravvolta, gabbia, o cappelliera?*
> *sovrasta i ciechi tempi come il flutto*
> *arca leggera—e basta al tuo riscatto.*

It will have to do, that. It will have to do. The house you bring with you, cage or hatbox? When they were too little to swim in the ocean, the children played Marco Polo in the bay. We had floats for them, a dinosaur, a shark; they paddled by the shore, under, over the waves. They shouted, Marco, Marco, and Polo, Polo! I am a mermaid, said Pom. The water was too hot, it was too cold. From *The Travels of Marco Polo*: "They accustom their cattle, cows, sheep, camels and horses to feed upon dried fish." It is a chapter about the Abyssinians. A is for Abyssinia, A is for Alastair, C is for Caroline, D is for Daniel, L is for Louie and you. On the Serpentine, Madame de Vionnet, in a little bark, *un canotto*, passes under a bridge and disappears. What does Madame de Vionnet see in front of her face? Lambert Strether. As we watch, the boat goes under a small arched bridge and capsizes. Although the river is—what is the word, not searched, something else, dragged? *Trascinato*, no body is found. It is a small boat. Let's call it the *Peapod*. It is a canoe, but smaller, trimmer: the size of the nutmeg wood canoes in New Guinea. It is not made of nutmeg wood; it is made of balsa wood and a kind of neoprene, which must not sit too long in the sun. In Siena there is a painting of this boat, by Sassetta. Not neoprene. No. But how do I get there from here? "You can imagine what fun I am having dreaming these wild dreams," wrote Michael, "and creating earth-shattering hypotheses." The two native boys swam three miles to shore; the next day when Wassing was rescued, Michael was missing: I think I can make it, he said. When they found Wassing, the boat was twelve miles from shore. "My weekly word is now 'inscrutable,'" wrote Patsy. And signed her letter, "Beware of yourself." I had pictured it as a narrow river, but that turns out not to be true. Just now, a flash of crossing Third Avenue. And then crossing Seventy-Second Street in the rain late at night for the first time with you. Starting and stopping. And, or. How far are we from sure? The boat like an eggshell, exposing what is mortal and unsure.

Beware of yourself. I began writing this to have something to show for—it—as I knew it would end, and now it is ending, or has ended, and I go to these pages for consolation, to hear your voice, to tell you a story, and there is no consolation. *Mi dispiace*. One of the first things one learns to say—*I'm sorry*—as in any language there is always so much to be sorry for. A is for ———. Didn't I start that way? A, my name is A———, and my husband's name is A———, and we come from Akron, and we sell apples. *Veniamo da Ancona e vendiamo anguille.* Enough rope to hang myself. Very good. But you do not like eels. No. Once, near Baltimore—what were we doing there?—there was an eel farm, the eels swarming under the boat. It was horrible. They looked like coiled copper-wire bracelets, covered in slime. Broken heart syndrome, or takotsubo, named for the way the left ventricle of the heart can suddenly weaken when one is heartbroken; the expansion of the muscle looks like the pot Japanese fishermen use to catch eels. Death by fire, water, ice, air. But what I didn't know when I wrote these pages is that love is elastic, that every place one is is the center of the maze. Later, I would imagine a past rather than a future because I knew better that the boat is always just this instant setting out from the shore; the waves are unreliable territory. From Martin Luther King: *Dear Governor, I want you to know that my thoughts are with you constantly since Michael's disappearance.* A hail of shrapnel.

Here is an email, now three weeks old—

Dear Caroline, amore mio, hope your drive to the seaside went smoothly and you are enjoying the children and what surrounds you. For me, busy days with more drama and problems than anticipated, and yet it moves. I am resisting calling when I miss you most. I remember shortly after spending our first time together telling you I felt "stupefied." And now I find "When Northumberland told Jane that she was queen, she fell to the ground and wept. She later wrote that the moment left her stupefied." With ardor, Lorenzo

In the blue notebook: *It seems clear that ornamentation varies from village to village, or perhaps more accurately from artist to artist.* A boy who was lost, a boy who loved beautiful things. Patsy wrote: *Do you ever think about who you are to other people? That is, can you let people see what you are feeling without, well, making yourself vulnerable? But maybe it's a-ok to be vulnerable? And how do you know if they like you just for yourself? There's a kind of horrible inscrutability about it. I felt it in Cambridge, a kind of whispering bubbling under the surface.* Remember me, when this you see. To thee the reed is as the oak. Michael's tutor at Harvard wrote: *If he had been less than who he was the loss would not have been so great, which compounds my sorrow.*

○

I say, you are something that happened to me. When years later you come to Rome, where I am staying for a few weeks in a dingy apartment steps from the Piazza San di Cosimato, I say, *che ci fai qui?* and you say, where else? It was the tail end of the plague. I have an idea we can be friends, I say. As always, you say, *hai troppe proposte*—you have too many ideas—but we cannot be friends. Why, I ask. Because you are a protagonist in my life. Rome deserted, the Piazza Navona turned into a dog run, no one in the Forum but ghosts—Pom at ten in her blue coat running among the tombs. And now the phone rings; it is you, or it is not. *Dimmi,* you say. I step out of the taxi, and there you are. You call from the train and ask if I will be home later. I am home now, I say. I come in an hour, you say. So come, I say, or, it's late, maybe tomorrow. I can't, tomorrow. What is love? It's not hereafter. I thought: for you, nothing is ever enough, so the choice is nothing. But it is not nothing. Please don't understand me too quickly, said Gide. We round the bend in our little boat; our own voices wake us from our long intimacy, jealous of it, as if it had a life all its own that we careened into and then shamefully backed away.

What he saw was exactly the right thing—a boat advancing round the bend and containing a man who held the paddles and a lady, at the stern, with a pink parasol. It was suddenly as if these figures, or something like them, had been wanted in the picture, had been wanted more or less all day, and had now drifted into sight, with the slow current, on purpose to fill up the measure.

I do not know—what I think? That is a start, then. Start there. *Iniziare qui.* Could this be the end? It falters? Yes. Roll the dice, roll the ball back, sweetheart. I want to make a note here. Yes? I saw your email before I left but I pretended I did not see it. The email upset me. I was dejected, by your sentence: that this week was busy. I do not want you to tell me ever again that you do not have time for me. It is not something to write to me after three weeks of silence. In that no time, I vanish. Where is the Caroline I am with you? Gone. And as I was going down to the city with Frank for a few days, and in fact if not exactly in spirit, I did not feel it would be proper to contact you or respond in a way which would embroil us in these last weeks of summer. Splitting hairs. This week, forest fires in Sierra Nevada. Perhaps we should not do anything that leads to dying. But what does not? I did not look at my email in New York and will look at it this morning: I do not imagine you will have written. A river of silence, a dugout canoe. *See that tin can? It doesn't see you.* But I am going to send you a package this morning, from the post office here: since you have a skirt, a blouse, a sweater, and knickers and so on, I am sending you shoes and stockings, so that if I want to get dressed after I have washed my hands at the sink, I will have what I need. I will get dressed and be the person you want me to be. In the meantime perhaps you will keep them for me. I will finish writing this letter—I want it to be done before I see you again, before the fall and its bloodthirsty leaves, and then, whatever happens, I will not write it down. At least not now. I will make the bed in the early morning, and take Pom to school. I will take account of myself. I will settle myself on the three-legged stool. There, I will say to myself, there, there.

Now we are in the dog days, the time of Sirius. And the Pleiades showers. Stars falling on the lawn: the children next door waving their sparklers by the woodpile and over the fireflies. A mirror of heaven. When the children were small, I would swim a mile in the bay every day, and Louie would stand on the sand and weep. This afternoon I went out to buy corn, and when I returned and parked the car by the boxwood, there was Pom with a scrape on her leg, and George was spreading peanuts to lure the wild turkeys who have taken up residence under the house. Louie had left her bicycle in a heap. But where was I? says Meredith. You have left me out completely! You were grown up, I say. There was little you wanted to hear then, from me. That will be a story for another day. The dragonflies have returned, settling on the parched butterfly bush, whizzing above the house like arrowheads. What will the wedding supper be? Two fried eggs and a bumblebee. *I am having the most wonderful time*, wrote Michael. Tomorrow is going to be a hot day, but soon the shadow of the dune will stain the beach up to the waterline. It will be chilly in the late afternoon, too cold to swim. A few windfall apples under the tree by the hedge. *The tornado set him down. It was the day after the Fourth of July, and he wasn't going to see the other side of Christmas.*

But—I must finish what I started here.

# ACKNOWLEDGMENTS

Again, for reading and rereading, and for conversation, thanks are due to Karen Balliett, Turner Brooks, Michael Cunningham, Edwin Frank, Sophie Haigney, the late Elizabeth Kramer, Katia Lysy, Jane Mendelsohn, Ludwig Olshansky, Marco Pasanella, Julien Rubinfien, and Susan Wiviott. To the Lopud Island Foundation, for time and space. At Farrar, Straus and Giroux, to Jonathan Galassi, Oona Holahan, and Scott Auerbach. To Sarah Chalfant and Luke Ingram at the Wylie Agency, manifold gratitude.

**Permissions Acknowledgments**

Grateful acknowledgment is made for permission to reprint the following material:

Lines from "Homage to Mistress Bradstreet," from *Collected Poems: 1937–1971* by John Berryman. Copyright © 1989 by Kate Donahue Berryman. Reprinted by permission of Farrar, Straus and Giroux. All rights reserved. Poem was initially published as a stand-alone book-length poem under the same title by Farrar, Straus and Giroux in 1956.

Lines from "Baltimore," words and music by Randy Newman. Copyright © 1977 Six Pictures Music (ASCAP). All rights reserved. Used by permission of Alfred Music.

"The Dove," from *Death of a Lady's Man* by Leonard Cohen. Copyright © 1978 by Leonard Cohen. Used by permission of The Wylie Agency LLC.

Lines from "A Liuba che parte," collected in *Tutte le poesie*, by Eugenio Montale. Copyright © 2015 Mondadori Libri S.p.A., Milano. Published by arrangement with The Italian Literary Agency.